Mommy's Cuddles

Zara knew what she liked as an ABDL, and she knew she wanted an MDLG relationship. What she didn't know was that finding the perfect Mommy is hard

By Tina Moore

Table of Contents

Chapter 1

Zara just wanted to cry. It wasn't as though there was anything particularly troublesome or difficult in her life. The clients she had spoken to that day were okay. Her boss was okay and left her alone most of the time. Fiona had even told her that her outfit looked nice after a meeting, which was high praise coming from her. But something was very wrong, even if Zara couldn't put her finger on it.

Maybe I am just feeling a bit overwhelmed in general, like there's nothing specific, but something is wrong, Zara thought to herself. She had finished work for the week and walked down the main street, wishing she could blink and be home. She walked down the busy street, which was filled with bars and restaurants, and deeply inhaled as she smelt the delicious smells.

I know what I need, Zara thought, turning the corner and walking into a Chinese restaurant, hoping that the soul-warming food would bring her comfort. She ordered her usual spring rolls and cashew and chicken dish, before sitting down and waiting for her order to be made. While she waited, she watched the people passing by, all seeming to have somewhere very important to be or something to do that could not wait. Zara had always loved to watch people. She wondered if she liked to watch them so she could learn how to behave in particular settings. As Zara sat there, she remembered how, when she was younger, she would go to the beach and watch how girls would flirt with boys as they played volleyball, wondering how it seemed to come so naturally to them. Nothing seemed to come naturally for Zara, and her mouth twitched as she looked down at her lap. Taking out her phone, she checked the time and knew that her favorite tv show would be starting soon and smiled as she heard her name being called.

"Perfect, thanks," Zara said as she took the paper bag and walked back out onto the street. She had noticed that when she was in one of these moods, where she felt like the simplest of stares would make her burst into tears, she would act tough. Really, tough. A lot tougher than she was, and she would glare people down until they got out of her way. She had learned that she had an aggressive type of resting bitch face and one which people often wanted to be away from, which suited her just fine.

Opening the door to her apartment, Zara flung her keys in the bowl on the hallway table and kicked off her heels, instantly sighing. Her heels acted like a trigger that when she put them on, her adult costume was complete and that when she took them off, she could finally be her little self. Zara walked to the kitchen, took a fork from the drawer, and sat on the sofa. She knew that she didn't have time to change before her show started, so bringing her knees up to her chest as she ate, she turned on her cartoons. It was during these times where she wondered what it would feel like to have a caregiver. She had watched all the vlogs, subscribed to all the online communities, and read all the stories about loving, tender, comforting Mommies but wondered why none of them seemed to want her as their own.

"I'm cute, right, Ducky?" Zara asked her stuffed duck, which sat next to her. She slightly smiled that she had, for a moment, genuinely thought her stuffie would reply. Shrugging her shoulders and biting into her spring roll, Zara watched her cartoons.

Argh, I've just got so many things on my mind, Zara thought to herself as she rubbed her temples. Although the weekend had been lovely, as she stayed in her blissful, little space, she still didn't feel rested as she sat in her office cubicle at work. The day was dragging on, and as Zara looked at the clock on her computer screen, she cringed.

Another six hours of this shit, she thought to herself, deciding to get up and make herself her third coffee for the morning. She walked passed the office gossips, wondering how they kept their jobs when they only did the bare minimum, reaching the refreshment station just as she saw Fiona come to stand beside her.

"You are going to give yourself a heart condition if you keep drinking coffee like this," Fiona, her colleague half-jokingly said. Zara just rolled her eyes and laughed.

"Well, anything to get me out of this place," Zara replied, stirring in the milk. She walked back to her desk, sat down, and sighed.

This is going to be a long day, she thought before continuing to work.

"Hey, we are all going out for some drinks after work. Apparently, there is a really cool band playing in a really shitty bar," Fiona said to Zara as the end of the day neared. Zara tilted her head, it was only Monday, and she thought it was humorous that they would go drinking so early in the week. She knew all the 'cool' people at work went to bars and clubs on a Friday after work, but she had never been invited. She didn't fit in with their 'look.' While she was naturally beautiful, Zara didn't feel the need to wear makeup or figure-hugging clothes. She preferred to be comfortable and relaxed.

"Okay?" Zara replied, unsure of what Fiona was trying to say, making Fiona roll her eyes.

"So, do you want to come with?" Fiona replied, spelling it out for Zara. Zara thought about the diaper and onesie which awaited her at home. She wasn't about to tell Fiona that, though. Fiona was the hot one at work. Every workplace has one, the ringleader of the 'cool' group. That seemingly untouchable woman who everyone either wants to be or wants to be with and Fiona was that woman. Zara thought it was odd that Fiona was trying to flirt with her, her battering eyelids, and the way her eyes smiled when she looked at Zara made her feel uncomfortable about the attention.

"Yeah, sure," Zara said, finding it hard to turn down a night out, smiling at the wide grin Fiona gave her.

"Great," Fiona said, practically bouncing away.

The bar was loud. Louder than Zara would have liked it to be. It was an unusual spot for young business and law employees to go. Still, they had transformed the smelt of stale beer into the smell of air conditioning, cologne, and money which hit Zara like a slap in the face as she walked into the bar, instantly regretted her choice.

Great, now I have to stay for at least a drink, she thought to herself, fake smiling as Fiona turned around and grinned at her. They found a tight corner and ordered some drinks, Zara grateful that her other colleagues had also decided to come because it meant that she didn't have to say too much. Zara was very good at faking laughing at their jokes, bopping around to music she hated, and generally looking like she was having a good time while wanting nothing more than to leave. Zara had become very good at blending into crowds. She often wondered if people even knew that she was an introvert because she masked it so well.

"Are you having fun?" Fiona asked. Zara could hardly make out the words, but nodded her head and gave a wide grin.

"Yeah, so much. Thanks for inviting me out," Zara replied, making Fiona roll her eyes.

"Come with me," Fiona said, taking Zara by the hand and walking out the back of the bar. The fresh night air hit them, making Zara feel light-headed almost instantly.

"Woah, I needed to get out of there," Fiona said, as Zara found a crate to sit on.

"I thought you were having fun," Zara said, pulling her coat around her.

"I was having about as much fun as you were," Fiona replied with a knowing look on her face. Zara smirked.

"I see," she said as Fiona sauntered toward her. Zara knew that having the hottest woman at work like you had its perks, but she also knew that Fiona wouldn't be able to give her what she wanted, she just didn't seem to be that type of woman that made Zara feel a connection.

"So, I saw the way you were looking at me," Fiona said, taking Zara's hands in hers. Zara sighed and bit her bottom lip.

It's probably a terrible idea to start something with her, Zara thought to herself as a gust of wind made Fiona stumble forward and into Zara's arms.

"Well, you're gorgeous," Zara said, beginning to blush despite the battle raging in her mind.

Maybe some harmless fun is a good thing. It's been ages since anyone has shown an interest in you, Zara thought, leaning forward to kiss Fiona on the lips. Fiona smiled into the kiss, wrapping Zara up in her arms and making Zara moan softly.

"Wanna get out of here," Fiona asked, breaking the kiss just long enough to speak. Zara nodded her head, feeling Fiona take her hand in hers and lead her out onto the street.

They walked quickly, Zara grateful for the pace, hoping that the alcohol would stay in her veins, she felt like she needed the liquid courage.

This is what normal people do, she told herself. Zara had always kept her little side a secret, ashamed of what someone might say if she told them. She certainly didn't want to tell Fiona. Zara imagined the most beautiful woman at work, laughing at her, and it made her cheeks blush red. As they neared Fiona's apartment, Zara inhaled deeply before stopping and kissing Fiona on the lips, wanting the hit of adrenaline to pump through her once more. As Fiona grabbed at her, Zara smiled, hearing her fumble with her keys as she struggled to open the door. Breaking the kiss long enough for Fiona to unlock the door, Zara giggled and followed her inside. She dropped her coat and bag, biting her bottom lip as she grabbed at Fiona's shirt, ripping it off.

"Wow, a little more passionate than I thought you'd be," Fiona said as she took off her bra and continued to walk into her room. Zara just smirked.

"There are a few things you don't know about me," she replied, taking her pants off and walking into Fiona's bedroom. Fiona lay down on the bed, now naked and backlit from the moonlight coming through the window.

"Why don't you show me then," she said, reaching out to Zara, who smirked. Zara lay on top of Fiona, feeling the warmth of her body before kissing her lips and snaking her way down her body, enjoying the wetness of Fiona's pussy as she stuck out her tongue and slowly licked her.

"Oh yeah," Fiona moaned, placing her hand on the back of Zara's head and pressing herself onto her mouth. Zara knew that Fiona would cum quickly as her moans filled the bedroom. Somewhat dissociated, Zara flicked and sucked Fiona's clit, fingering her at the same time as she came hard, almost surprising Zara. She hadn't realized that she was in her own world, somewhat forgetting that she was having sex, which made her laugh.

"Oh my god, it's usually so awkward the first time, but that was amazing," Fiona said, flipping Zara onto her back, just for Zara to push her off slowly. She didn't want to make Fiona feel rejected.

"I don't really feel like it. I kinda just want to snuggle," Zara said, worried that Fiona would think she was strange or something.

"Yeah, sure," Fiona said, lighting a candle and cuddling up to Zara, who was already almost asleep.

Chapter 2

"Breakfast?" Fiona asked, waking Zara up. Zara blinked her eyes open, realizing that she had fallen asleep for the whole night and that it was, in fact, a work morning.

"Oh shit," Zara said, hurrying out of bed and putting her clothes back on.

"I can't. I have to go home and change. I can't go to work in the same clothes as yesterday," Zara explained, annoyed that she had let herself stay the night.

"You can just wear some of my clothes," Fiona said, walking to the closet and placing a bowl of yogurt and fruit down on the night table closest to Zara.

"Eat," Fiona said, taking Zara by surprise at the tone in her voice as she picked up the bowl.

"So, this could look cute. You can have a shower, and then we can go to work together,"

Fiona gleefully said, making Zara roll her eyes. Fiona had a way about her that made everyone fall in love with her almost instantly, and Zara, being as stubborn as she was, had decided to deliberately not fall for Fiona's charms. That, however, was proving to be quite a challenge.

"Thanks for this," Zara said, standing up after she finished her breakfast and walked into the bathroom. She ran the hot water and stood under the tap. This was not the first time that Zara had felt torn up inside. She could feel her little self begging to come out, but as she rubbed shower gel over her breasts and stomach, she shook her head to try and refocus.

Getting out of the shower, she wrapped a towel around herself and walked back into the bedroom. Fiona was sitting on the edge of the bed, waiting for her.

"So," Fiona said, making Zara nervous.

Did I talk in my sleep? Oh god, what is she going to say? Zara thought in a slight panic.

"So?" Zara calmly replied, getting dressed

and trying not to break out in a sweat of uncertainty. Fiona took her time to get up, slowly walked over to Zara, and kissed along her collar bone.

"So, do you want to be my girlfriend?" Fiona asked, making Zara freeze.

"What?" Zara questioned, unsure if she heard correctly, laughing as she looked Fiona in the eye.

"Do you want to be my girlfriend?" Fiona repeated, laughing that she had shocked Zara.

"Um," Zara said, turning back around and continuing to get dressed.

"I have wanted to ask you for ages. How has everyone else in the office noticed me flirting with you, except for you?" Fiona said, Zara, sighing.

She is stunning. It's not the way I thought I'd find a girlfriend. It's a bit soon. You do like her, though, Zara thought to herself before picking her towel up from the floor.

"Yeah. Okay," Zara replied, kissing Fiona full on the lips, giggling at her squeal of delight. Fiona let her go and happily walked into the kitchen, leaving Zara alone in the bedroom.

"This was not how I thought my week would go," Zara quietly said out loud as she finished getting dressed in somewhat of a daze.

Fiona and Zara caught the train together, made subtle remarks to each other at work, but decided to go to their separate apartments that evening.

"I just really need to be in my own space for a while, babe," Zara said to Fiona in their lunch break.

"Yeah it's cool, I get it," Fiona said, somewhat disappointed that Zara wouldn't be coming over. Fiona always did this, as in got really attached to a girl super quickly. Zara, on the other hand, liked to take her time and really get to know someone before committing to them, which made her wonder why she had agreed to be Fiona's girlfriend in the first place.

"Thanks, I just like, my own bed and stuff," Zara said, kissing Fiona on the cheek before getting up to go back to her cubicle. She could hardly wait to get home, and she spent the next four hours fantasizing about what it would be like the moment she walked through the door.

These awful heels are coming off. I am taking a bath with bubbles and my duckies. I am going to put nuggies in the oven and my cartoons on. I'm going to wear the thickest diaper, and cutest onesie and my milk is going in a bottle. I am going to color and play and build my block towers, Zara thought as she typed away at her keyboard, realizing that for the first time in almost 24 hours, she was genuinely smiling.

Zara took the train home, walked quickly to her apartment, and sighed as she closed the door behind her.

"Thank fucking goodness," she said out loud, sighing as she kicked off her heels and shook her whole body, trying to almost shake the day out of her system. She stripped her clothes off as she walked to the bathroom and dumped them in the wash basket, before turning on the tap. She put the plug in the bath and squirted her pink, glittery bubble bath into the water and watched as the room became a steamy haze of sweet-smelling pink mist.

"Yes, this is what I was looking for!" Zara exclaimed as she lowered herself into the water, instantly feeling better. She slunk herself down and under the water, enjoying how being completely submerged made the world outside become quiet. She re-emerged and smiled to herself.

Maybe not everything is as bad as it feels, Zara thought to herself, playing with the bubbles. She dunked them into the water, tried to make shapes out of them, and splashed around until the water was cold and the mist had long faded. Getting out of the tub, she wrapped herself in her unicorn hooded towel and walked out into the kitchen. Taking out a tray, she set her nuggies out and put them in the oven before she walked into her bedroom and laid down on her bed.

"What should we wear, Ducky?" Zara said out loud, rolling over and taking her duck stuffie in her hands and wrapping her arms around it.

"That's what I thought!" Zara exclaimed, jumping up and walking to her cupboard and taking out a diaper, baby powder, and a light purple onesie. Zara quickly diapered herself, zipped up her onesie, and hung her towel in the bathroom before going back to the kitchen and checking on her nuggies, Ducky, in tow.

Chapter 3

Zara knew that things were going too fast as she approached her desk on Wednesday morning. The big give away was the dozen long-stemmed roses that were elaborately displayed in an elegant box. The other was the champagne and chocolates that proceeded to appear upon her arrival. Zara blushed as her colleagues looked on wistfully, not noticing that while this may have been their fantasy, it wasn't Zara's. As she opened the card which accompanied the gifts, she couldn't help but appreciate that this gesture was what most people would want. That Fiona was simply trying to seduce her, without knowing her well enough to know what would actually work.

I hope you have a beautiful day, sweetheart. I can't wait to see you tonight, read the card, making Zara frown.

What is happening tonight? She thought,

racking her brain to try and remember if she had made a plan, remembering nothing.

"You got them then?" Fiona suddenly said, seemingly coming out of nowhere. Zara gasped, wondering how many more surprises she could handle.

"Yeah, I did. Thank you, everything is really lovely. But, maybe next time, a little more, low key?" Zara said, squinting as she said the words, not wanting to offend Fiona but trying to set up a boundary.

"You deserve more than low key. That's why we are going here," Fiona said, missing the subtle hint and making Zara bite her bottom lip, slightly annoyed.

"Where?" Zara asked, holding out her hand to accept the paper invitation that Fiona was waving. Zara looked over the flyer and tilted her head to the side.

"Fiona, really? I have nothing to wear to something like this," Zara said, rolling her eyes and handing it back to her before turning around in her chair.

"Okay, well, we don't have to go. What do you want to do instead?" Fiona asked, scrunching up the flyer and throwing in the trash. Zara thought for a moment, knowing fair well what she wanted to do and smirking to herself before deciding that telling Fiona that she wanted her to Mommy her all night would be way too much.

"Do you want to get take away Mexican and watch a movie at mine?" Zara offered, raising an eyebrow. Fiona, who clearly had to lower her expectations as to what she was expecting to do that evening, nodded her head before leaning forward to kiss Zara full on the lips, making Zara's eyes go wide.

"Text me your address. Oh, what? Nobody cares that we kiss," Fiona said, winking at Zara before getting up and walking away.

I fucking care! Zara thought to herself as she angrily turned around to face her computer screen.

Zara had spent the rest of the day wondering if she would bother to text Fiona her address, but at 4:30 in the afternoon that Fiona called back into Zara's cubicle and spun her office chair around.

"So, what time do you want me to come over?" Fiona asked, sitting on the edge of Zara's desk and folding her arms across her chest.

"Like, 7?" Zara said, writing down her address on a post-it note and handing it to Fiona.

"Okay. Sorry if I rushed you or something," Fiona said, taking the note and putting it into her pocket. Zara gave her a heartfelt smile, standing up and straddling Fiona's thighs as she embraced the other woman.

"I'm not like the other girls here," Zara softly said, kissing Fiona's cheek. Fiona looked at her with sad eyes and nodded her head.

"Yeah, I know, that's what I like about you," Fiona replied, wrapping her arms around Zara.

"Then, you'd know that I am quiet, I like, I don't know, quiet stuff," Zara laughed, enjoying how Fiona looked at her.

"I'll keep that in mind next time I decide to announce us to the entire office," Fiona replied, feeling guilty for making Zara feel uncomfortable.

"Thanks," Zara answered, sitting back down in her chair.

"See you tonight," she said, glad when Fiona took the hint and left her alone to finish her work.

What the hell was I thinking!? Zara thought as she whipped around her apartment, trying to hide any trace of her being a little.

Oh, great. Come over Fiona, just excuse all the cartoon themed pillows on my bed, Zara thought, collecting them all and throwing them into her cupboard before turning around and searching for anything that didn't seem fitting for a 29-year-old's room. Rolling her eyes to herself and shaking her head, she kicked Ducky under the bed as she saw his little tail sticking out.

"Sorry, Ducky," Zara whispered as she left her room and continued to de-little her apartment.

I need to stop buying so much stuff, Zara

thought to herself as she put her princess printed blankets in the storage chest that she used as a coffee table.

"Okay. Good," Zara said out loud to nobody, trying to reassure herself but feeling like she was about to cry just as a knock came from the front door. Running to the door, she opened it and smiled as she saw Fiona.

"Low key enough?" Fiona said, opening her arms to show Zara her outfit. Fiona had her navy sweatpants on, her flip flops, and a gray hoodie over the top of a tight white t-shirt. Her red hair was in a messy ponytail, and she wore natural makeup. Zara smirked, she hadn't thought that Fiona owned anything apart from high-end luxury fashion brands and definitely didn't think she owned any natural-looking makeup. It was a stark contrast to her usual, almost runway model makeup she wore at work.

"Yeah, perfect," Zara replied, smiling excitedly and moving out of the way, so Fiona was able to walk inside, closing the door behind her.

Fiona walked to the middle of the living room and stopped, turning around to face Zara.

"Come here," she said, taking Zara's wrist and pulling her to her as Fiona wrapped her arms around Zara and kissed her passionately, taking her by surprise.

"So, dinner?" Zara said, breaking the kiss and pulling away, making Fiona laugh.

"You sure do know how to keep me on my toes. Rejected twice in one day," Fiona said, only half-joking. Zara sat on the couch and took out her favorite take out menus.

"I'm not rejecting you. I am starving," Zara replied, glad when Fiona sat down next to her.

"So, which is your favorite?" Fiona asked, looking through the various Mexican menus. Zara felt herself give Fiona a little smile and promptly corrected herself before answering.

"I like these guys. They are a bit authentic, though, do you mind? Or do you like more mainstream?" Zara questioned, her big eyes looking up at Fiona.

"Authentic is good," Fiona replied, taking out her phone.

"I'll ring," she said, dialling the number of the restaurant, unknowingly making Zara fight to not fall into little space as she watched Fiona take control. Fiona ordered, paid over the phone, and hung up, delighted that Zara had moved closer to her.

"Do you want to snuggle together when we watch the movie?" Fiona asked, almost causing Zara to clap her hands.

"Yeah, sure, whatever, if you like," came Zara's response trying to act cool, making Fiona laugh.

"We don't have to," Fiona said, trying to read Zara.

"Yes, I want to," Zara quickly said as she moved next to Fiona and wrapped her arms around her waist, making Fiona laugh.

"Okay, cool," she said as they began the movie and waited for their order to arrive. Zara tried to steady her heartbeat as they watched the film, as Fiona started stroking her arm gently.

She doesn't even know what she is doing to me! Zara thought so loudly she was worried that Fiona might hear. As Zara slowly turned into Fiona, Fiona looked down into Zara's eyes and winked at her.

"Do you want a blanket?" Fiona asked, noticing that Zara was cold, breaking their embrace and lifting the lid off the coffee table.

"No, I!" Zara exclaimed, jumping up and thinking she was about to pass out.

"What?" Fiona said, taking out one of the princess blankets from the wooden chest and draping it over her body, holding up the corner of the blanket and looking at Zara innocently. Fiona tried to hide her amusement as she watched Zara try to maintain her composure and sit back down, rigid and her breathing shallow. Fiona and Zara watched the film for a while, Fiona wondering how to approach the huge elephant in the room.

"Baby?" She softly said, making Zara's eyes go wide, and she turned her head slowly to face

Fiona.

"Hmm?" Zara said, trying to act like she wasn't sitting under her princess blanket with the hottest woman who had ever been interested in her as they waited for their Mexican take out and watching a movie.

"Baby. It's alright. You don't have to pretend that you don't love this," Fiona said, indicating to the blanket.

"I don't know what you want me to say," Zara softly said, looking down and feeling deeply insecure.

"I like it," Fiona said, causing Zara to look up and wonder just how much of her private world she wanted to let Fiona into.

Maybe this is how you get a Mommy? Zara thought to herself, as the doorbell rang, causing Zara to jump up and answer the door.

Well, that sucked, Fiona thought to herself, wishing that Zara would just open up to her. She had been looking for a baby girl for years, always seeming to scare them off. She wasn't sure what it was about her that was so off-putting to them. Sure, everyone seemed very interested in the beginning, but as they got deeper into a relationship with her, no one seemed to like her at all.

It's probably the hair, everyone says redheads have no soul, Fiona thought to herself as she saw Zara come back and place their food on the coffee table.

"Do you need any help," Fiona called from the living room as she saw Zara flutter into the kitchen to get glasses and plates.

"No, I'm good," Zara said, coming back to the living room and setting their food up.

"Can I pour you a drink?" Fiona asked, taking out the bottle of soda she had ordered as Zara nodded her head. Fiona picked up the glass, beginning to pour but then put it down suddenly, turning to look at Zara.

"Look. I know you're a little. I'm a Mommy. I can see it!" Fiona confessed, making Zara's eyes go wide as she slowly packed the paper wrapping into the bag and placed it on the floor.

"Oh, okay," Zara replied, unsure of what the correct response.

"Good, that's out in the open now," Fiona said, somewhat impressed with herself. They turned the movie back on and ate in silence, both wondering what it would take to make the awkward silence and energy of the room disappear.

She is beautiful, the type of woman like anyone would want to be with. She's a great kisser. She doesn't care that you're a little because she is a Mommy for Christ sake, what is your problem?! Zara thought to herself as she stared at the television, too nervous to look at Fiona.

"This is so awkward," Zara suddenly said, bursting out laughing, making Fiona laugh as well.

"I know," Fiona said, putting her head in her hands and shaking her head.

"What were we thinking?" Zara said, turning to face Fiona as she brought her knees up to her chest.

"We have zero chemistry!" Fiona exclaimed, clapping her hands as she emphasized her words.

"I know!" Zara replied, rolling her eyes.

"But like, you are so gorgeous. I should feel something, but I just don't feel it," Zara added, shrugging her shoulders.

"Oh, I feel the same way. It's just so hard finding a little, you know? You want to take every chance you can get," Fiona said, laughing when Zara shook her head.

"No, not really," Zara replied, smirking and making Fiona give her a look.

"So, you want a beer or something?" Zara asked, suddenly feeling the stress of the evening fading and feeling more herself.

"Yeah, absolutely," Fiona said, getting up to follow Zara into the kitchen. She held the door open for Zara, who turned to look at her, with the same expression Fiona had written all over her face.

"I mean, you're already here, it would be a waste if," Zara slowly said as she put the drinks down and kissed Fiona, enjoying the sound of Fiona slamming the fridge door shut. Pushing her against the kitchen bench, Fiona pulled her hoodie off, her shirt coming off in the process.

"Can I pull your hair?" Fiona said between kisses, smiling as Zara nodded her head.

"Let me hear it, baby," Fiona said as she grabbed at Zara's clothes, ripping her shirt off and turning her around, pushing her down on the bench.

"Yes, pull my hair, but don't call me baby, call me sweetheart," Zara replied, not wanting to go into her little space too deeply.

"Good girl?" Fiona asked, biting her bottom lip as she kicked Zara's feet apart.

"Yeah," Zara gasped, feeling Fiona put her hands in her sports tights and feel her for the first time.

"Fuck yes," Fiona replied, pulling Zara's panties to the side and stroking her slit, coating her fingers in her juices.

"Push that ass out for me," Fiona said,

grinding against Zara's bottom as her fingers slowly entered her, making her moan and arch her back.

"So pretty," Fiona said, reaching forward and feeling Zara take her knuckle deep. Grabbing a fistful of Zara's hair with her free hand, Fiona felt her clit spasm as she looked at the beautiful woman under her control and moaned. Spreading her legs, Fiona grinded against one side of Zara's ass, feeling her clit being gently stimulated as she finger fucked Zara to orgasm.

"Oh fuck, sweetheart," Fiona gasped as she felt Zara coat her fingers, her cries of climax driving Fiona wild.

"Can I lick your pussy, sweetheart?" Fiona asked, wanting to taste Zara, who nodded her head and turned around, feeling Fiona rip her tights and panties off.

"So pretty," Fiona said, running her fingers through Zara's strip of pubic hair as she positioned herself under Zara's pussy, feeling her buckle forward as Fiona's tongue made contact with

Zara's clit.

"Fuck," Zara gasped, grabbing Fiona's head and pushing her face into her cunt as she lapped up Zara's juices.

"Yes, just like that," Zara moaned as she arched her back and let her body take over, surprised that Fiona could drive her over the edge with her tongue. Not many people had been able to eat Zara out till orgasm. Pushing Fiona away, Zara grabbed the edge of the bench and held herself up, gasping as she kept Fiona away with her foot when she tried to come back for more.

"I'm done," Zara said, laughing as she shook her head and rubbed her pussy gently.

"That was fun," Fiona said as she got up, taking the beers, opening them, and placing one in Zara's hand before toasting and drinking it as she walked back into the living room. Zara couldn't help but admire the lithe body Fiona had as she drank her beer topless.

"You have really nice tits," Zara said, drinking her own beer after putting her panties back on, making Fiona laugh.

"You want to see them?" She offered. Zara seriously considered it for a moment.

"Nar, I'm good, I don't want this to get any weirder," Zara laughed, Fiona nodding her head, understanding where Zara was coming from and putting her shirt back on, before sitting on the couch next to Zara.

"So," Zara slowly said, wondering how to move forward.

"Yeah. Um, we can just pretend like this never happened if you want. Or we could I don't know, um, hang out sometimes," Fiona suggested making Zara laugh.

"It's okay. You don't need to babysit me, I'm good," Zara replied, smirking as she took her princess blanket and wrapped herself up in it.

"Alright. I didn't want you to think I was just using your body or something. I liked fucking you, though," Fiona said, finishing her beer. Zara smiled.

"You did?" Zara asked, taking Fiona by

surprise.

"Yeah. Why would you think I didn't?" Fiona replied, turning her body to face Zara.

"I don't know, I just sort of think that people don't notice me or find me attractive or whatever," Zara said, trying not to sound like she was fishing for compliments.

"I mean. You definitely hide yourself, but anyone would have to be stupid if they couldn't see your beauty," Fiona genuinely said, making Zara's heart flutter.

"Cool," Zara replied, her go-to response for when she felt happy but didn't know what to say.

"Cool," Fiona agreed, smiling at Zara.

Chapter 4

"Hey," Fiona hissed at Zara the next day in the office. Zara couldn't believe that it was only Thursday.

This week is next level crazy, she thought to herself as she looked around and saw Fiona standing by the elevators. Zara shrugged her shoulders at her, wondering what was going on that required such secrecy.

"You said this wouldn't be weird. Guess what, this. This is weird!" Zara softly exclaimed as she huddled over what Fiona was trying to show her.

"Weird, fun. It sort of all just blurs into one at some point," Fiona replied, causing Zara to scoff at her.

"Anyway. Here, there's an event, wanna go?" Fiona asked as Zara looked at her phone screen.

"What? Like, together?" Zara replied, confusion written across her face.

"No! Well, yeah, I mean. We could go together, but not like together together," Fiona replied, making Zara laugh.

"Yeah, okay. I hate doing to things by myself anyway so, why not," Zara said, surprised at how quickly she could make a decision. Usually, she would have freaked out about doing something new and outside her box of "normal." Still, something about the way Fiona was able to maintain a completely neutral dynamic with her, made Zara respect her, trust her even.

"Sweet. Pick you up at 8?" Fiona asked, making Zara laugh.

"I'll make my own way there, but meet you out the front?" Zara quickly replied as the elevator doors opened before she scurried away.

"Looking good!" Fiona said, making Zara laugh. Zara wore a tight black dress, a flannel button-down tied around her waist, fishnet stockings, and black combat boots. Her hair was out and perfectly straighten, and her natural makeup completed the look.

"Thanks, I didn't really know what I should wear, so I figured this would work," Zara replied, smoothing down her dress over her torso.

"It definitely does! I would have thought you'd go for something, a little more girly. With all your princess stuff, I just thought," Fiona said, shrugging her shoulders.

"I just wasn't feeling all cute and girly tonight," Zara replied, before quickly giving Fiona a look.

"Anyway, why do you care? We aren't going to this, together together, remember," Zara said, sticking her tongue out and making Fiona laugh.

"Fair point," Fiona replied before walking toward the entrance of the convention center.

"Have you seen this before?" Fiona asked, holding the door open for Zara.

"Only in movies," Zara replied, walking into the hall and seeing the woman skating around the track. The sounds overwhelmed her, and she found herself feeling small and wishing that she could reach out to hold Fiona's hand, forcing herself to resist the urge was more difficult than she had realized.

"Wow, so this is roller derby!" Zara said as she saw a woman being hip-checked.

"Pretty cool, huh?" Fiona said, sitting down and watching the bout.

"How did you know about this?" Zara said as she watched, smiling as the crowd cheered.

"I saw a flyer, the one I took a picture of to show you," Fiona replied, before cheering with the crowd. A player on the yellow and black team caught Zara's eye, and she felt her eyes glaze over. The woman was tall, her blonde hair had pink tips, and she moved through the pack with ease and speed. It almost looked like ballet instead of roller derby. Her athletic form was highlighted by the spotlight, which followed her around the track, and as she raised her arms in victory and the crowd cheered wildly, Zara cheering along with them.

How do I even talk to her?! Zara thought, as the woman passed her in the stands and winked at her, making Zara's stomach lurch and knot.

"That's Gill. Everyone actually calls her by her first name because she doesn't need an alter ego, she's made such a name for herself in the derby circuit, she doesn't need a scary name to threaten anyone, Gill is enough," Fiona explained, making Zara blush.

"Oh yeah, everyone thinks she's amazing, don't worry!" Fiona said, sensing that Zara was already under Gill's spell.

"Is she single?" Zara found herself suddenly saying, making Fiona laugh and taking her by surprise.

"I don't know, go and try to shoot your shot when the bout's over!" Fiona encouraged. Zara was surprised at how confident she had been feeling lately.

Maybe it is because Fiona knows I'm a little and I don't have to be worried about her finding out coz she's into this as well? Zara thought, deciding that it didn't matter why she was feeling so self-assured, she liked it, and that was all she was going to allow herself to think about the matter.

The bout ended with Gill's team losing by 3points, much to the crowd's disappointment.

"Boo!" Zara yelled when one of Gill's teammates was sent to the sin bin, allowing the opposition to gain the win.

"How could they call that!?" Zara yelled at Fiona, making Fiona laugh.

"I think I made you a fan," Fiona laughed as the crowd in the stands began to leave.

"Hey, you want to grab a drink?" Fiona asked, Zara, having to think for a moment before shaking her head.

"I think I might hang around for a while," Zara replied, a knowing smile forming across her face, causing Fiona to smirk.

"Alright, get it, girl!" Fiona said before waving goodbye and walking away. Zara turned around, taking a step just to bump into someone.

"Oh my gosh, sorry," Zara said, taking a step back to see who she had crashed into.

"It's fine," Gill said, causing Zara's eyes to go wide and her mouth to gape over.

"I, I, just watched you play," Zara said, shaking her head when she realized how stupid she just sounded, relieved when she saw Gill laugh.

"I know, I saw you, watching me play," Gill replied, enjoying Zara's cute choice of words. As an awkward silence came between them, Zara began to play with the sleeves tied up around her waist.

"You want to come and get a drink?" Gill asked, Zara, trying to subdue her excitement.

"Yeah, I heard that there was an after-party," Zara said, referring to the announcement she heard come over the speakers.

"Oh. Yeah, I didn't mean that. It'll be too loud, and I won't be able to hear you speak," Gill replied, making Zara smile. After a big night, she was happy with the idea of going somewhere quiet.

"Yeah, that sounds nice," Zara replied,

smiling.

"Okay, give me 15minutes to get showered and presentable, and I'll take you out. I'm Gill," Gill said, extending her hand, Zara realizing for the first time that she hadn't introduced herself.

"Oh, I'm Zara," she said, shaking Gill's hand, noticing how small it made her feel as she closed her hand around Zara's.

As Gill went to get ready, Zara sat on the bleachers and flicked through her phone. There was nothing particularly interesting on her social media accounts, but it was better than having to dodge eye contact from strangers.

"There you are," Gill said as she approached Zara, starling her.

"Oh honey, I didn't mean to scare you," Gill affectionately said, hoping that Zara didn't mind the more nurturing side that she often chose to ignore.

"It's cool," Zara replied, shrugging her shoulder and trying not to get lost in Gill's eyes. They had a circle of navy around the outside, with hazel green in the middle and little flecks of gold reflecting from the lights, almost taking Zara's breath away.

"Ready to go?" Gill asked, placing her hand on her sports shoulder hand and running her fingers through her almost dried hair. She had washed it to get the rank smell of derby sweat out of her hair but hadn't bothered to dry it off completely. Zara nodded her head, and Gill fought herself not to grab the younger girl's hand and lead her away, instead, tilting her head and gesturing to Zara to follow her out of the arena.

On the street, people were still milling about, watching as Gill and Zara walked in silence passed them. Zara noticed that they all seemed to stare at her as she walked by, making her feel uncomfortable. Gill noticed, wondering how to best comfort Zara, not wanting her to be freaked out and reconsider getting to know her.

"So, tell me about yourself," Gill asked, as they turned a corner. Zara always hated this part of getting to know someone. She always wished that she had interesting hobbies or cool stories to tell. She thought for a moment before looking up at Gill, who could sense that there was something important Zara was about to say.

"So, I'm 29, I work as a success coach, and if you really want to end up with me, you should know I'm a little and if that isn't cool for you, then let's just stop right here," Zara said, almost feeling sick as she continued to walk. She never had, in all her nine years of identifying as a little, said it out loud, especially not to someone she had only just met.

"I don't know what that is," Gill said, lying. She had some idea of what it was but didn't want to assume and get Zara's hopes up.

"For me, it's a lot of age play," Zara said, not wanting to get into it too deeply. She was still reeling for saying it out loud. Gill stopped walking, and Zara thought that she was going to turn and run.

"We are here," Gill said, indicating to Zara to go inside as she opened the door. Walking into the bar, Zara ordered a shot of vodka and a beer before walking away from Gill and finding a chair. She was sure Gill would follow her but needed a moment to get her head around what she had just done.

This is so typical of you. Everything is going fine, and you have to go and do something that makes you feel all fucked up again, Zara angrily thought to herself as Gill came to sit down in the opposing chair.

"So, if you were to explain it all to me in three sentences?" Gill asked, taking a sip of her beer. Zara crossed her legs on the chair before she looked at Gill, who was patiently waiting for her to respond.

"So, it's a sub-category of BDSM. It can be sexual or non-sexual, and comes in a whole lot of experiences and *flavors,*" Zara said, surprised at how easy it was becoming to talk about her kink. Gill raised her eyebrows and nodded her head, making Zara glad she hadn't scared her off.

"Well, there you go," Gill said, processing it

to the best of her ability.

"Did something happen to you as a kid or what?" Gill asked, taking Zara by surprise.

"Um, no, not really. I just like how it feels to be looked after," Zara replied.

"So, like, you're not like, depressed or something?" Gill continued making Zara scoff.

"What? I just know a lot of girls who are subs are a bit fucked up," Gill said, as Zara tried not to be insulted.

"That's not very tactful," Zara said, finding it interesting that she was correcting Gill. She would have never spoken up about how something made her feel in the past.

"I don't really do tact. I'm not trying to insult you, I just don't sugar coat stuff," Gill said, seeing the way Zara pulled back from her.

"I can appreciate the honesty, but no. That's the misconception out there that bottoms, generally, are damaged, or something has gone wrong for them, but it's not the case. People, at large, have their shit, I think bottoms are just better at talking about it, in my experience," Zara said, looking around the bar and wondering why Gill had a smirk on her face.

"I agree. I guess I would identify as a top, and I constantly push my past and shit down, so no one sees," Gill said, taking Zara by surprise.

"So, what's your story then?" Zara asked, coming to sit down next to Gill and look her in the eye.

"Well, when you look at me like that, how can I refuse to answer?" Gill said, placing her hand on Zara's thigh.

"I work in a casino, it's pretty basic, but it's fun. I have a cabin in the mountains that I go to in the wintertime. I never knew my Dad. He died in a motorcycle accident before I was born. My Mum remarried this prick who kicked me out when I was 16 because that's when I came out, and I've been on my own ever since," Gill said, finishing her beer and getting up to go to the bar.

"That's heavy," Zara replied as she approached the bar and bought her second drink.

Gill just turned to look at Zara, surprised at how her defences seemed to come down around her.

No girl has ever been able to do this to me before, Gill thought as she reached out and touched Zara's cheek affectionately.

"I feel so weird around you," Gill laughed before going back to sit down, taking Zara by the hand as she did so.

Chapter 5

"Well, this is me," Zara said as they approached her apartment. Gill would have usually taken a girl back to her house and be kicking her out by now, but she and Zara had talked all night. When they were kicked out of one bar because it was closing, they went to the casino and sat on the slot machines, not to play, but to chat. It hadn't felt right just to hit and quit on Zara, and as the sun rose behind her, Gill knew that Zara was somebody special.

"I'm going to read up on littles and ABDL," Gill said, wanting to keep Zara for as long as she could.

"What was the other one you said?" Gill asked as Zara beamed up at her.

"MDLG," Zara said, hugging Gill spontaneously and quickly walking up the stairs to her apartment. She was worried that if she stayed holding onto her any longer, she would melt into Gill's loving embrace.

"Okay, bye," Zara said as she opened her door and walked inside. She was exhausted. Not only because she had stayed awake all night, but because she had spoken about just about everything she had ever done. It wasn't that extreme feeling when she had met toxic partners in the past. Those ups and downs were like a roller coaster from hell. With Gill, it was calm, balanced, and even though they had not been able to say goodbye to each other until the early hours of the morning, it felt aligned.

Zara locked the door of her apartment and slowly undressed herself. She kicked off her boots, leaving them by the door and untied her shirt from around her waist. She walked to the bathroom and dropped it in the wash basket, pulled off her dress, and rolled down her fishnets, taking off the ankle socks she wore underneath. She turned on the water to the shower before she took off her bra and panties and closed her eyes as she stood under the water and sighed.

Well, that was unexpected, Zara thought to herself as she felt herself begin to relax under the pressure of the hot water.

Gill could hardly wait until she got home to begin looking up all the things she and Zara had shared. She liked the Zara didn't make her feel stupid for asking what felt like 10,000 questions.

She's certainly not like other girls. Gill thought to herself as she crashed onto her bed. Despite her desire to sleep, Gill stayed up searching MDLG, ABDL, littles, middles, bigs, looking at photos of events, following accounts, and joining pages online before finally falling asleep at 9:30 that morning.

My sleep schedule is going to be fucked up for days, was the last thing she thought before falling into a deep sleep.

Gill woke up to the sound of construction works outside her bedroom window and blinked her eyes slowly awake.

Fuck, what time is it? She thought to herself, grateful that she had the day off. She felt around the bed for her phone, remembering that she had been researching Zara's kink before she fell asleep. Finally, finding it under her pillow, she checked the time and smirked to herself. It was late afternoon. Groaning, Gill got up, had a shower, got dressed, and went to the kitchen. She opened her fridge and remembered that she needed to go to the grocery store, before rolling her eyes and slamming the door shut.

This is bullshit, she thought to herself as she grabbed her keys and headed out the door.

Gill walked down the street, trying to remember all the things she needed to get, but finding that her mind was elsewhere. After hours of searching, she had images of diapered women, playrooms, and all things adult-baby related running through her mind. She wondered what sort of play Zara enjoyed, how a relationship would look with her, and if she would ever feel like a Mommy.

She's so cute. I want to be with her, but I don't know if I can give her what she wants, Gill thought to herself as she entered the store. She absent-mindedly put things into her shopping cart. She imagined punishing Zara for breaking a rule, enjoying the image of her being strap on fucked and forbidden to orgasm.

Gill paid for her groceries and took out her phone on the way back to her apartment. She hoped that she wouldn't wake Zara up.

"Hey, it's Gill, from last night, and this morning actually," Gill said down the phone, surprised at how nervous she was when talking with Zara.

"Hi," Zara said, having only just woken up five minutes earlier, she hadn't bothered to call in sick, she just assumed they would figure it out when she didn't turn up.

"I hope I didn't wake you?" Gill said, concerned that she had disturbed Zara.

"No, it's cool, I was up. How are you?" Zara said, snapping Gill back into the confident person she was usually.

"Good. I was just thinking about you," Gill said, making Zara smile.

"That's nice," Zara replied, getting up out of bed and walking out to her balcony.

"Yeah, so, do you want to meet up sometime again? I read up on everything we talked about last night, and I think it could be really fun to explore that with you," Gill said, squinting and biting her bottom lip, hoping that she wasn't overstepping.

"Um, yeah, I mean. That could be fun to show you the stuff I like. Do you want to come over tonight for a few hours, maybe come at six?" Zara said, feeling very proud of herself for the suggestion.

"Yeah, that sounds great," Gill replied, hanging up the phone and feeling herself getting hyped up.

Zara had spent the two hours before Gill arrived getting ready. She tided the house, took out some of her toys and laid them on her bed, and practiced what she would say to Gill. She got ready, deciding to put on her baby doll dress and her hair in a messy ponytail, and white ankle socks. Then she sat on the couch and waited, for what felt like an eternity. She was just about to lay down on the couch when she heard a knock coming from the door and excitedly jumped up and ran to it.

"Hey," Zara said, opening it up to see Gill standing in front of her.

"Hi. You look cute," Gill answered, smiling down at Zara, who blushed.

"You wanna come in?" Zara asked, stepping back and allowing Gill to enter her apartment. Gill walked in, standing awkwardly in the living room, making Zara laugh.

"You can sit down if you like," Zara said, causing Gill to look at her and sit bashfully.

"So, you didn't hate what you discovered?" Zara asked, sitting down next to Gill, immediately putting her at ease.

"No, in fact, I kind of liked it. From like, the

Mommy perspective," Gill said, blushing as she replied.

"Wow, that is really cool. Do you have any questions or?" Zara replied as she shifted in her seat.

"Yeah, heaps," Gill said, surprising herself. She had always been a more dominant type of woman, but this was different. It seemed to bring out in her a softness that wasn't familiar to her. Sure, she could imagine controlling and disciplining Zara, but the gentleness and care that coupled those feelings were strange and new but exciting to her.

"Like, how do you like to have adult relationships? What does a typical day look like for you? How do you balance what you need to do as an adult and still have enough time for age play? What do you look for in a Mommy, just to name a few?" Gill asked, looking at Zara seriously. Zara laughed. She hadn't expected this to go so well when she had told Gill, she was a little. It was a selfish act, something she was only doing for herself. She hadn't thought that Gill would be interested in it, or her after she had told her. She just wanted to say it out loud without any repercussions.

"Well. I guess I have adult relationships like everyone else. Sometimes things that people do trigger the little side of me and it comes out a little bit, but mostly I find it easy to keep both sort of separate, I just prefer to have them separate, it makes it easier for me to enjoy both. A typical day looks like me getting up and going to work. I like to have little time at night and on weekends, and that's how I balance, making sure that I have everything that I need. What I look for in a Mommy. I haven't ever given it much thought because I've never had one before. But I guess someone I'm compatible with! Everything else is just extra. Like, if we have that chemistry, and have a good foundation of friendship, I guess the relationship will progress naturally. Oh, I don't want to feel rushed, that's probably one of the big ones," Zara explained, enjoying that Gill was clearly listening. That was one of the things that Zara liked about Gill. Whenever Zara spoke, Gill gave her her undivided attention and didn't seem to listen just to reply, but really tried to understand where Zara was coming from. Gill took in the words Zara had said, nodding her head as she digested them.

"That sounds like, really standard actually. So, it's kind of like, for you, it's about having work and life balance, and then age play is what you do to unwind and relax and enjoy experiencing?" Gill asked, making Zara's heart swell. She loved how Gill seemed to see her.

"Yeah, exactly," Zara said, beaming. Gill nodded her head as she understood.

"So, do you want to show me some of the stuff you like?" Gill asked, somewhat timidly making Zara giggle.

"Yeah, come on," she said, taking Gill's hand and leading her into her bedroom. She sat on her bed and patted the spot next to her.

"Have a seat," Zara said, watching as Gill

looked over the things on her bed.

"What were you expecting?" Zara laughed as she saw Gill's face.

"I don't know," Gill laughed, looking at the blankies, stuffies, and adult pacifiers. Zara hadn't put out everything she liked, just a few things so that Gill wouldn't get freaked out.

"So, this is cute. You're just like a little girl in a sexy, grown body, huh?" Gill said, making Zara roll her eyes.

"Yeah, kinda," Zara replied, watching as Gill picked up a pacifier, playing with it.

"What other stuff do you like?" She asked, looking at Zara. Zara got up and opened her cupboard, letting Gill see the collection of diapers, onesie, and cute AB dresses and accessories. Gill got up and flicked through everything, looking at Zara when she was finished.

"I would have never guessed this," Gill said, making Zara nervous.

"Why not?" She asked, fearful that Gill wasn't as into it as she thought she would be.

"Because look at you!" Gill replied. Zara looked down at herself. It was true. She did look like a fashion model when she put in effort into her appearance, but that was what she loved about being a little. She didn't have to impress anyone, and no one expected anything from her. It was enough for her just to be herself. She had long learned to hide how gorgeous she was, disappointed that it seemed only to bring her misery when someone became interested in her. She had become comfortable with wearing little to no makeup, having her hair in messy buns or ponytails, and wearing baggy clothes. But when she was a little, she could be her naturally beautiful self because nothing bad could happen to her.

"Yeah, I know. That's what I like about being a little. I can look how I look, and no one expects anything from me. All I have to do is be a good girl," Zara said, feeling herself beginning to enter her little space being around all her things, she had to admit, it was very space triggering.

"So, you come home, have a shower or something, and then this is what you dress in around the house? Being in little space?" Gill asked, wanting to know how it all worked.

"Pretty much. I go to the gym after work on most days or go swimming. Then I come home, shower, put dinner on, and then I can start to get into my little space and only get out of it to do the dishes or put the washing on, for example. Sometimes on the weekend, I don't feel super little, but I still like to wear a diaper, I just like how they feel," Zara said as she closed her cupboard door.

"Do you use them?" Gill asked, sitting back down on the bed.

"No, I just like wearing them," Zara replied, coming to sit next to her. Gill nodded her head, and Zara was happy that she didn't seem too phased by anything she had just seen.

"So, I'm just going to come out and say it. I'd really like to be your girlfriend," Gill said, making Zara laugh.

"What?" Gill said, tickling Zara involuntarily, making Zara giggle.

"Yeah, I kinda thought that we were both wanting that, that I was just showing you all this stuff so that you could make sure you wanted to be with me," Zara replied, crossing her legs.

"Oh. Well, good then," Gill laughed, realizing that she wasn't telling Zara anything new.

"I know it's kind of like, doming from the bottom, but you might need to help me like, make sure that I'm being a Mommy, the right way," Gill nervously said. Zara thought it was adorable that Gill was nervous, but didn't feel like teasing her for it.

"There's no right way to be a Mommy, but I get what you mean. I can show you, in time," Zara said as Gill nodded. She liked that Gill wasn't trying to rush into anything. It made Zara feel safe and calm.

"Do you want to watch a movie?" Gill suddenly asked, Zara's eyes going wide.

"Yes!" She exclaimed, her little side coming

out and making Gill smile. She shifted on the bed, clearly wanting to ask something but not knowing how to form the sentence.

"Just ask," Zara whispered, tilting her head down to look up at Gill, who was now blushing.

"Do. Do you want to take a blankie or paci or something?" Gill asked, biting her bottom lip. Zara nodded her head, grabbed her paci and princess blankie before taking Gill's hand, and putting her paci in her hand.

"You can put it in my mouth whenever you want," Zara said, looking at Gill with her biggest puppy dog eyes. Gill smiled, suddenly feeling her nerves shift and slowly pushed Zara's paci into her mouth, looking at her and feeling a new, strange sensation washing over her.

"You look really, sweet," Gill said, taking a moment to look at Zara before smiling in surprise.

"Come on," Gill said, standing up and holding out her hand to Zara, who eagerly took it. They walked out to the couch, and Gill sat down, letting Zara work the tv remotes.

"This feels really different. Like all soft and kind and cute and stuff," Gill said, surprised at how easy it was allowing herself to feel all the feelings of love, softness, and non-sexual affection.

"I'm glad you like it," Zara replied, letting Gill wrap the blankets around them both as Zara snuggled into her side. They started the movie, and Zara felt like she was in heaven. Gill's larger, soft yet athletic body made the perfect pillow, and as the movie progressed, Zara could feel herself falling asleep in Gill's arms. Much to Gill's surprise, she knew that she never wanted to let Zara go. She wanted her, craved her, and believed that no one could take care of her the way she could. It was a strange sensation to experience, so soon after meeting someone, yet one which she welcomed. As Gill looked down to see Zara clutching at her breast, sound asleep, Gill smiled and carefully reached for the tv remote, turning the tv off. She gently placed her arms under Zara and carried her like a princess into her bedroom. Pulling back the sheets, she placed Zara in bed, brushing the hair off her face as she stirred.

"It's alright, honey. You're safe. You're in bed," Gill whispered as she tucked in the stuffies that were on the bed around Zara. Gill looked down at Zara and smiled to herself. She loved that Zara had dared to open up to her so quickly, grateful to be allowed to look after another woman with such tender care.

This has always been me. I just never knew what it was called, Gill thought as she walked back out into the living room and sat down on the couch. She thought back on her past relationships and saw many similarities between what Zara was looking for and what she naturally gave. Her ex's had always loved her dotting and affectionate ways, but they always found that she wanted to do too much for them. One woman had even told her that she felt like her independence was being taken away. That comment still stung. It wasn't that Gill tried to be overpowering, it was just that, she wanted to make sure that her partner was taken care of to the highest degree. If a girlfriend said she needed new shoes for work or sport, Gill wanted to be the one to get them for her. If they said they didn't like their hairstyle anymore, Gill found the best hairdresser in their neighborhood for them. If they needed doctors' appointments, she organized it. She had dated sugar-babies before, thinking that would satisfy her need to look after someone, but they were really only interested in her money and not her.

But this, this just feels so right, Gill happily thought, taking out her phone and scrolling through content as she waited for Zara to wake up.

Chapter 6

Zara woke up with a start.

What happened? She thought, looking around her darkened room. She remembered that Gill had come over and they had watched a movie, gasping when she realized that she had fallen asleep as the movie had begun.

Oh my gosh, how embarrassing, she thought, getting up and seeing her stuffies all around her. Zara tilted her head, not giving it a second thought as her feet touched the ground, and she smelt the smell of fresh herbs and cooking coming from her kitchen. She walked out of her room to see Gill was still here. In fact, she was in the kitchen, cooking something which smelt delicious.

"Hey, sweetie, I thought you might be hungry after your nap," Gill said, spinning around to see Zara looking at her, a mix of shock and excitement on her face.

"I don't know what to say," Zara said, sitting down on the bench stool and watching Gill.

"I hope this is okay? I didn't just want to leave you," Gill said, stirring the pot on the stove.

"This is great. You're so lovely. You didn't have to do this though," Zara said, smirking as Gill passed her a bottle filled with water.

"You haven't had enough water today," Gill said, gesturing to the bottle. Zara liked that Gill seemed to be in her natural element, but what surprised her the most was that she felt as though she and Gill had been in a relationship for years. Everything seemed to flow so effortlessly.

"Here you go," Gill said, placing a bowl of warm beef stew on the counter in front of Zara. Zara was surprised. She had never had beef stew before but knew that it would become one of her favorites as the meat melted in her mouth.

"Oh fuck yes, this is amazing!" Zara said, making Gill laugh and frown at the same time.

"That's enough of that language, young lady," Gill teased, kissing Zara's cheek before getting up to get a drink for herself.

"You know, this feels really nice," Zara said, as she watched Gill. Gill smirked.

"Yeah. I can't believe I only met you a day ago. This feels right," Gill replied, causing Zara to smile in sheer happiness. She couldn't believe her luck. It all just seemed too good to be true.

"I feel the same way," Zara said as Gill sat next to her and began to eat dinner.

"I'm actually having a really hard time not jumping into this with you," Zara said, enjoying dinner. Gill laughed before looking at her.

"I know. Me too. But I don't want to ruin it by rushing in," Gill added, making Zara nod her head. She knew that she needed to take her time, let the relationship unfold naturally, but she just couldn't help but fantasize about how it would feel to be playing with Gill.

"Don't worry, I'm not going anywhere," Gill said, reassuringly.

Zara took leftover dinner to work on Monday,

hardly being able to hide her smile as she walked through the office.

"Oh, somebody looks happy," Fiona said as Zara sat down in her chair.

"Do you just loiter around my desk, waiting for me to come in?" Zara laughed as she turned on her computer.

"No," Fiona scoffed, mildly offended. She moved to the edge of Zara's desk and crossed her legs, her thigh-split in her skirt, exposing her toned leg.

"Was she as good as me?" Fiona teased, making Zara roll her eyes.

"We didn't have sex," Zara said, taking Fiona by surprise.

"What do you mean?" Fiona asked, crossing her arms over her chest.

"We talked," Zara replied, turning around to face Fiona, who was trying to understand.

"Oh, wow. Well good, that's what you wanted, somebody to take things slow with you. Good, I'm happy you found someone like her then,"

Fiona said, standing up.

"Fi," Zara softly said, sensing Fiona's disappointment. It was obvious now that Fiona was still interested in Zara, even though it had been awkward between them.

"She doesn't have your tits," Zara said, shrugging her shoulder and smiling as she saw Fiona perk back up, before winking at Zara and walking away. Zara just sighed and rolled her eyes. She liked that Fiona was who she was, but she wasn't the right person for Zara, and as heartbreakingly stunning as she was, she knew that truth deep in her soul.

Hey honey, I hope you have a good day. I saw this and wondered if you would like it? Came a message from Gill as Zara tried to get refocused on the mountain of work she had to get through. Looking at the picture she had sent, Zara gasped, as she saw the big, soft, multicolored Llama that Gill had sent.

Omg, YES!! Replied Zara, being barely able to control her excitement, smiling down at her phone, much to Fiona's disappointment. She had been watching Zara from her office, wondering what was so good about Gill that Zara wanted her as badly as she did.

Is it just because Zara said no? Am I just being possessive? It's not like we had any chemistry or anything. We both agreed that we aren't right for each other. Is it just coz I know she's a baby? Is it because I could get anyone I want, so I want the one person who doesn't want me? Fiona thought to herself as she angrily typed on her keyboard, wishing that she could shake the feeling of rejection from her bones.

Chapter 7

Zara went over to Gill's house the next weekend, excited to see her again after days of only messaging.

"Hi," Zara said as soon as Gill opened the door, jumping into her arms and snuggling in close as Gill wrapped her arms around her.

"Hi cutie," Gill replied, enjoying how it felt to have Zara's body pressed against hers.

"I'm glad you could come over," Gill said, taking a step back and breaking their embrace. Zara beamed up at her, melting her heart and finding it hard to keep her mind from wondering. Zara's body made her wet, but she knew she didn't want to scare her off and so cleared her throat and shut the door before leading Zara into her space.

"I guess this is how nervous you were when I first saw your place," Gill said as she looked back at Zara, who followed her.

"Yeah, a little bit," Zara said as they reached the back porch, and Gill gestured to Zara to sit down.

"This is really lovely," Zara said as she looked out over the backyard. The wooden porch had fairy lights strung up along one side, a hammock was set up next to a fire pit on the grass, and there was a garden bed with colorful flowers.

"Your place is really nice," Zara said, looking at the cake Gill had made as she cut her a slice.

"Thanks. It's not much, but it's cute, and the rent is cheap," Gill said, sitting down and pouring herself and Zara coffee.

"You don't seem like that, no-nonsense roller derby queen when you are off the track," Zara said, before taking a bite of the moist cake, savoring the flavor.

"I like derby because it gives me an outlet to be somebody I'm not usually. Like, I am pretty relaxed, but my ego still comes into play from time to time, and derby lets me be that center of attention, outspoken, loud, aggressive, and passionate, without it being a bad thing or upsetting anyone," Gill said making Zara smile.

"I like that. I like that you know yourself so well," Zara said, sipping her coffee. Gill sat back in her seat and tilted her head back, enjoying the afternoon sun on her face.

"You're really pretty," Zara said, biting her bottom lip as she finished her slice of cake. She ran her finger over her bottom lip, leaned back in her seat and pushed her pussy out toward Gill.

"I don't think you're ready for me," Gill said, excited that Zara had initiated sex.

"I'll be the judge of that," Zara said, standing up and walking over to Gill, just to straddle her lap, wrapping her arms around her neck and feeling her breasts against hers, making Gill's clit throb.

"Such a naughty little girl," Gill whispered, grabbing Zara by the back of her head and pulling her hair, making her moan.

"Fuck me, Mommy," Zara whispered in Gill's ear, causing Gill to spread her thighs, and take one of Zara's hands from around her neck and pushed it into her pants.

"First, you're going to give Mommy a reason to," Gill sensually said. Zara was surprised. Usually, she didn't have to do too much to be fucked, but she liked that Gill made her work for it, it made it feel more special. Gill put her hand over the top of Zara's and guided her fingers around her clit and into her pussy, holding Zara's hand there as she pushed herself forward, wanting Zara deeper inside of her.

"Nice and slow. Take your time," Gill said, bringing Zara's mouth down on top of hers. Gill reached under Zara's dress and smirked when she felt that Zara wasn't wearing any panties.

"Dirty little thing," Gill said, gently parting Zara's pussy lips and rubbing her knuckle over the girl's sensitive clit, enjoying how she shuddered as she was teased.

"Oh, does the baby like that?" Gill teased, flicking Zara's clit, making her gasp each time. Zara just closed her eyes and moaned as she felt Gill coat a finger in her pussy juices, before slowly sliding it inside of her. Gill was still working Zara's hand over her own cunt, smirking as she felt Zara struggle to focus as she was toyed with.

"Did Mommy say you could stop?" Gill whispered into Zara's ear as she filled her with a second finger, curling her fingers and anchoring Zara to her lap.

"No," Zara moaned, as Gill rubbed her clit with her thumb.

"No, Mommy," Gill corrected, feeling Zara's pussy clench as she heard the words.

"No, Mommy," Zara replied, beginning to grind on Gill's lap, desperate to cum. Gill smiled in satisfaction as she leaned further back and watched as Zara ached to cum, deciding that she was going to have to wait a little longer.

"I don't think you've done enough to deserve an orgasm, baby girl," Gill said, smirking as she pulled her hand from Zara, enjoying that look of disbelief on her face.

"Oh, don't worry, I'll show you exactly what

you need to do to cum," Gill teased, shaking her breasts for Zara, who was speechless. She knew that the level of admiration she felt toward Gill was dangerous when she had to stop herself from saying that she would do anything Gill wanted.

"Tell me what I need to do, Mommy," Zara said, moving her body how Gill wanted her. Gill cradled Zara in her arms, moved one of her legs up on the table, the other one wrapped around Gill's leg, being held open and exposed. Gill wrapped an arm around Zara, supporting her head as her other hand lifted the hem of Zara's dress, uncovering her from the waist down. Her lips were open, her wet, pink pussy on full display. Gill pulled her top down, letting her breast fall out of her bra and pushed her nipple into Zara's mouth.

"Mmm, just like that," Gill said as she felt Zara begin to pull on her nipple with her soft lips, her tongue making it hard. Gill replaced her nipple with her fingers and watched how Zara made them wet before pushing her nipple back into the girl's mouth and sliding her fingers back into her pussy in one slow motion, making her moan.

"That's it," Gill said, as she saw Zara's eyes roll back. Zara wrapped her arm around Gill's body, her other one gripping Gill's thigh as she was fucked. Gill loved how Zara thrust up to meet her fingers as they reached her hilt, aching to be given release. Gill looked down. This is how she had fantasized about Zara. The beautiful woman, filled and at her mercy.

"Please let me cum," Zara gasped, her clit hard and throbbing, her cunt dripping wet.

"I shouldn't hear girls with Mommy's nipple in their mouths," Gill said, taking her fingers out of Zara and putting her heavy breast back in Zara's mouth before taking a toy from her pocket and sliding it up and down Zara's wet slit before beginning to tease her asshole with it.

"Just like we talked about. This is what you wanted, isn't it?" Gill said, referring to the multiple fantasies that they had shared over text message. Zara nodded her head, feeling the butt-plug press into her resisting asshole.

"Don't fight, Mommy," Gill said, holding it against her with her thumb and tapping on her clit with her fingers, making Zara tilt her head back and moan. She felt Gill add pressure, gasping as the butt-plug entered her, the pain mixed with the pleasure she was getting on her clit, making her head spin. Gill held her tight as she entered her pussy, making Zara buck her hips as she found her g-spot and refused to leave it alone.

"Should Mommy be mean and tell you that you can't cum, baby girl?" Gill whispered as Zara edged on the brink of orgasm. Zara's pleading eyes suddenly opened, and she looked desperately into Gill's eyes, hoping that she would be allowed to have what was sure to be a crushing orgasm.

"Mommy's not that mean," Gill said, bending down to kiss Zara, as her thumb began to work her clit.

"Cum for Mommy," Gill said, feeling Zara's body convulse immediately as she flooded Gill's hand and left out a high pitched cry before collapsing in Gill's strong arms, spent. Zara snuggled into Gill, burying her face in her ample cleavage before beginning to suck her thumb.

"Thank you, Mommy," Zara softly said, wriggling away from Gill's fingers, which were still in her pussy.

"Okay, little one," Gill said, taking the hint and taking her hand away.

"Do you need some downtime?" Gill asked, seeing Zara's little side for the first time. Zara nodded her head and stood up, her dress falling down as Gill smoothed it over. They had spoken about the kind of aftercare that Zara liked to have, and Gill had pre-emptively made sure she had everything that Zara had mentioned.

"Let's go inside. I can run you a nice bath," Gill said, taking Zara's hand and leading her into the bathroom. She gently undressed her, making sure to give her lots of cuddles as Zara became clingy and grabby. Gill took the butt-plug from Zara's ass and helped her into the bath. Gill turned the lights off, lit some candles, and sat by the bath, excited to be needed at the level she desperately required. She hadn't even considered that she needed to be a Mommy Domme before meeting Zara, but as Zara reached up for her, she knew this was exactly the type of relationship she had been searching for for so long.

"Mommy," Zara softly said, getting taken out of the bath and wrapped in a towel. She rested her head on Gill's breasts, her thumb in her mouth, and Gill tenderly dried her body. Zara was pleasantly surprised that she was able to go so deep into her little space, with Gill. Although she always seemed to keep a foot in both her little space and her adult space, being able to get into little space as quickly as she had made her happy.

"I've got you," Gill lovingly said, as she wrapped her arm around Zara and walked with her to her bedroom. She lay Zara down on the bed and went to her chest of drawers, taking out a diaper and onesie. Gill had never diapered another adult before but knew that it was something she wanted to do, especially because she knew that it would make Zara happy. She had seen videos on social media of Mommies diapering their adult babies and felt quietly confident.

"Really?" Zara asked as she saw Gill come back with the diaper in her hand.

"Yes, baby. What else would I put you in? You're too little for big girl panties," Gill said, finding that the words came from her mouth easily. She smiled. It felt nice to have so much control and authority in a relationship. Gill placed everything she needed down on the bed and began to lay the diaper out on the bed. She moved Zara on top of it, sprinkled powder over her, and made sure it covered her so that she wouldn't rub anywhere. Fastening the tabs, she enjoyed the feelings washing over her. She took the onesie, gently dressing Zara before sitting back and looking at her.

"You're really cute," Gill said, slightly unsure what to do next. Zara noticed and crawled over to Gill, hugging her tightly and nestling her face into Gill's neck.

"Can we snuggle together in bed, Mommy?"

Zara asked, laying down and half pulling Gill down with her.

"Of course," Gill said as she pulled back the sheets and turned off the lights.

Chapter 8

Gill was working double shifts for the next few weeks, as the floor was understaffed, which meant that she and Zara could only text and call. Zara didn't mind. She was happy the relationship was able to go at a slower pace and learn about Gill, without the ability to jump her bones.

"How was work?" Zara asked Gill on a Friday night. Gill had told her that she would call when she had time, but if Zara missed it because she was in bed or asleep or at work, that was fine. They had played phone tag for the last two days, and Zara had almost missed this call as well, having to jump out of the shower and run to her phone.

"It was fine. I am tired, though. I'm glad there is only one more week of this shit," Gill replied, pouring herself a drink and sitting down on the floor next to the floor to ceiling window, which overlooked the city.

"I bet. I'm sorry I can't come over and help you feel better," Zara replied, making Gill laugh.

"Shouldn't it be me looking after you?" Gill questioned, sipping her drink. Zara shook her head, even though Gill couldn't see her.

"No, Mommy, sometimes I can look after you too!" Zara exclaimed.

"Oh yeah, what would you do?" Gill said, finishing her drink and laying down on the carpet. Zara thought for a moment before smirking.

"First, I would take off your work clothes. Starting with your shoes and socks. Then I'd unbuckle your belt and pull your pants down slowly. I'd loosen your tie, unbutton your shirt and push you back on the bed in just your bra and panties," Zara said, making Gill undress herself the way Zara was describing.

"And then," Gill said in a husky voice, caught in the daydream of Zara's fantasy. Zara giggled and bit her bottom lip before continuing.

"Then I would slowly get on top of you. I'd

run my fingernails up your tummy and around your body, unclipping your bra and kissing down your collar bone until I reached your breasts. I'd gently grab them, playing with them and sucking on your nipples as my hand slid into your panties," Zara teased. Gill had run her hands down her body, following the path Zara was paving.

"Do you like it, Mommy?" Zara said, making Gill smirk.

"Yes. Keep going baby girl," Gill softly moaned, closing her eyes.

"I'd slowly part your lips, circling your clit and sliding my little finger into your pussy, knowing that you'd be wet enough. Then I'd play, doing nothing, in particular, just teasing you, feeling you. I'd kiss your inner thighs, licking your clit and sticking my tongue into your pussy, but nothing so constant that you could get off. I'd want to see how long I could tease you. How long I could play with you before you grabbed a fistful of my hair and held my mouth against you. Forcing me into you and grabbing at my throat until I gave you what you wanted," Zara said, stopping as she heard Gill's labored moans and gasps down the phone.

"I know you like that. I know you need me to look after you sometimes, Mommy," Zara said, hearing Gill's orgasm as she called her Mommy and smiled to herself, satisfied that she had given Gill pleasure.

"You are such a good girl," Gill said, opening her eyes, surprised that their phone call had turned out this way.

"Are you free tomorrow? I want to take you out for the day," Gill said suddenly. Zara frowned.

"I thought you said you'd be too tired. That you just wanted to sleep on your day off," Zara replied, as the rain began to pour outside.

"I thought I was going to be too tired too. But I suddenly have all the energy in the world," Gill laughed, hearing the rain.

"But maybe, we do something indoors. I can pick you up at ten if you'd like?" Gill asked, thinking of what she and Zara could do.

"Ten would be perfect," Zara said, smiling down the phone and hanging up.

Zara wasn't sure what she wanted to wear. She had taken a long shower, put on her fanciest lingerie and did her makeup, excited to try the new eyeliner she had bought earlier that week. She walked around her apartment, her hair flowing in the cool breeze as she sipped her coffee by the window seat.

This feels really lovely, she thought to herself, checking the time and running her fingertips over her soft skin. She looked out the window, watching as the people on the street hurried about their day. They always looked like they had so many important things to do, making Zara smile.

It's a Saturday, and I don't have to work, she thought, remembering how she used to spend her weekends before she had graduated from college. Back in those days, she worked at a fancy shoe store, selling only the highest quality of products.

She hated it there. The people were so entitled, the job was incredibly repetitive, and she could predict what her day would be like, months in advance. She knew she had to get out of there, but she had college, which meant that she had to stay working there for several years before she could leave. She still remembered her last shift. She had stolen a pair of shoes that she had always admired. She wasn't sure if it was because these were the most expensive shoes in the store or if she did, in fact, like them. All she knew was that she felt like she deserved them, and so she took them. She hadn't done too many other naughty things in her life. This was the biggest one. Zara smirked at how brazen she had been. It was a similar attitude she had when telling Gill that she was a little.

Sometimes, the juice is worth the squeeze. She thought to herself as she got up, finished her coffee, and headed into her bedroom. She took out her black stockings and pink dress, her black jacket, and those black heels she had stolen. Dressing herself, she looked in the mirror and knew that she looked good, just as she heard her doorbell chime.

"I'll be down in a minute," Zara said, pressing the intercom and quickly grabbing her keys, handbag, and heading out the door. Zara walked downstairs, opened the door, and stopped in her tracks when she saw Fiona standing in front of her.

"You're not Gill," Zara said, confused and tilting her head.

"Good observation," Fiona smugly replied, staring blankly at Zara.

"Well, um, what do you want?" Zara asked, knowing that Gill would be there any moment.

"I wanted to talk about us," Fiona said.

Clearly, things hadn't worked out between the intern, Zara thought, remembering how Fiona had been flirting with a particularly sweet new intern, before shaking her head and looking mildly angry at Fiona.

"There is no, us, Fi," Zara replied, annoyed that she thought there was a chance that they would be together.

"Yeah, I know that. But I think we just got off to a bad start. Everything is awkward at the start. I'd like to try again with you," Fiona said, just as Gill drove to a car space on the street.

"I don't, though. Sorry Fi, but I'm not interested in being with you. You're beautiful, funny, kind in a bitchy sort of way, which is really fun to be around, but I don't want to be with you," Zara said, looking at Fiona apologetically.

"I have to go," Zara said, smiling at Fiona pitifully before walking away and getting into Gill's car.

"Just drive, and quickly," Zara said as she sat down in the passenger seat, Gill following her request.

"What's going on?" Gill asked when they were around the corner. Zara had seen the excited look on Gill's face as she got into the car, feeling guilty that she hadn't been able to greet her the way she had planned.

"So, that woman I was with. Her name is

Fiona. We work together. Before I met you, we tried to be together, but it was just so weird and like, there was no flow, and it just sucked. But she wanted to try again with me. So I was just telling her that that wasn't going to happen," Zara explained, Gill putting her hand on Zara's thigh.

"Sucks to be her," Gill replied, making Zara laugh. She loved that Gill was so self-assured and didn't feel threatened or annoyed, and Zara reached for her hand, holding onto it tightly as Gill drove them to their first destination.

"Where are we going, actually?" Zara suddenly asked, realizing that Gill hadn't told her what they were going to be doing.

"Well! Now that you are here, I can tell you," Gill enthusiastically replied.

"We are going to do a few things today. And seeing as it's probably going to rain, I figured we should do the outside stuff first," Gill said, turning into the zoo parking lot.

"Love it, nice, good call. Can I get a stuffie?" Zara said, feeling herself drift into little space. Gill noticed, too, and smiled. She liked that Zara didn't try to hide herself from her.

"Only if you are a good girl and hold Mommy's hand," Gill replied, parking the car and getting out. Zara playfully skipped over to Gill after she got out of the car, delighting that there were only a few other people around.

"I guess not many people want to go out when it's overcast and rainy," Zara said, reaching for Gill's hand.

"No, which is perfect because it means there will be fewer people, more opportunity to be Mommy's baby girl," Gill whispered into Zara's ear. Zara giggled as they walked toward the ticket booth, Gill paying, and both of them walking in.

"I do think it's cruel that they cage up the animals, though," Zara said, looking at a jackal, noticing a bandage around its leg. Gill smiled.

"So do I. That's why I took you to this one. It's not like a normal zoo. It's a rehabilitation center. So, not all animals are here all the time. Like, I think I read online that there are no coyotes here at the moment because none have been brought in that need to heal. Only sick animals come here, and they stay only as long as they need to before being put back into the wild," Gill explained, delighting Zara.

"That is amazing!" Zara replied, happier to be here supporting the center.

They walked around the enclosures, looking at the animals and watching exhibits on snakes, flying foxes, and raccoons.

"I like that the lady said that even though raccoons are seen as a pest, that if an animal needs help, they provide it," Zara said as they looked at a bear who had been hit by a car. It had a bandaged side and was walking slowly towards a tree that had food strung up to it.

"Yeah, just like you. I still look after you, even when you are a pest," Gill teased, making Zara laugh.

They went to a food stand and bought hotdogs and soda before finding a spot underneath a tree that was dry.

"So, have you thought about what you want from the gift shop?" Gill asked, opening Zara's soda for her. She loved that she knew she could be her normal, caregiving self toward Zara without Zara feeling as though her autonomy was being taken away.

"Hmm, I think I just want a stuffie," Zara replied, snuggling into Gill as she ate her hotdog and watched a mountain lion being taken for a walk. It had a sore paw, and Zara watched as the handler walked slowly beside it.

"I think it would be really cool to work here," Zara said, imagining herself doing this job.

"Yeah, but just as you get attached to the animals, they would leave. I think I'm too much of a softie to do this job. I'd cry all the time," Gill laughed. Zara nodded her head, deciding that she would probably be just as emotional.

"But it would be so good because you would know that they are going back to the wild, where they belong. Animals don't belong in cages. Only for when they are sick and getting treated,"

Zara said, catching the way Gill was looking at her.

"What?" Zara whined, giggling as Gill continued to stare.

"Oh, nothing. You are just so cute. Come here, my little animal," Gill said, pulling Zara into her lap and holding her tight.

"Hey!" Zara giggled, Gill, letting her go and finishing her hotdog.

Gill and Zara spent far longer in the gift shop than either of them had expected.

"Mommy, I can't decide," Zara whispered in Gill's ear. Zara had gone around the store several times, narrowing her choice down to two stuffies. One was a mountain lion, and the other was a bear.

"I think it's sad that they get hit by cars so much that they have these available all the time," Gill said, more to herself than anyone else, as she watched Zara loop the store once more.

"Baby," Gill said, catching Zara as she walked passed her.

"Yes?" Zara said, wide-eyed, making Gill

laugh.

"Let's just get both. We have to get out of here. There are still things I have planned," Gill said, delighting Zara.

"Really?" Zara said, cuddling into her soon to be new stuffies.

"Yes, come on," Gill said, putting them on the counter before paying the lady.
Zara walked out of the zoo, cuddling both her stuffies. Gill gently put her seat belt on as Zara continued to play with them.

"I'm so happy you are having a good day!" Gill exclaimed, driving back onto the road.

"So, where are we going now?" Zara said as the rain began to fall on the windscreen.

"Wow, that was great timing," Gill said, turning on the heating.

"I'm surprised how cold it gets when it rains, it's icy," Zara replied. Gill reached into the backseat and grabbed the blanket that she had packed.

"I thought we might need this later, but I

guess you need it now, baby girl," Gill said, giving it to Zara. Zara snuggled into the thick blanket, warming up in seconds.

"So, where are we going now, Mommy?" Zara asked, yawning and turning her body to face Gill.

"The movies," Gill replied, making Zara's eye go wide.

"This really is the best day ever!" Zara exclaimed, clapping her hands in excitement.

Chapter 9

Zara was surprised how quickly the months seemed to pass by. Before she knew it, she and Gill were living together, had set up a dynamic that suited both of them, and were enjoying life at a level they hadn't thought possible. Zara's work with her clients had improved, and she felt as though she was able to understand them on a deeper level, especially where their relationship problems were concerned. Fiona had even settled down, having found herself another intern to occupy her time with, life was as close to perfect as it had ever been.

"Hey, hey," Fiona said, walking up to Zara at the refreshment station. Zara had taken to allowing Gill to decide what she wanted to wear, and it showed. Gill had taken her shopping for new work clothes, and Zara's slim-fitting skirt and plunging neckline knitted pullover had caught

Fiona's attention the moment she laid eyes on her.

"Hi, Fi," Zara said, amused that under different circumstances, she could have called Fiona, Mommy.

"You look nice. I see Gill has taught you a thing or two," Fiona playfully teased, noticing how Zara's makeup was significantly more flattering than usual. Zara just rolled her eyes at Fiona, making her laugh.

"What makes you think that I didn't do this myself?" Zara replied, stopping what she was doing and turning around to look at Fiona, taking small sips of the hot chocolate she had just made herself.

"I don't know. I just thought maybe you'd have given that up?" Fiona said, beginning to make herself a coffee.

"Given what up?" Zara asked, happy that she had someone to talk to who understood, to a certain extent, the dynamic of her relationship. She had always hated having to give generic answers when people asked her how Gill was when she knew they wouldn't be able to handle the truth.

"Given up power over your appearance," Fiona said, a wicked smirk on her face.

"No. This is for me. Gill does enough," Zara said, walking away just to have Fiona grab hold of her upper arm, causing her to look up in surprise.

"Just be careful with how much you give up, alright? I have heard she has a propensity for demanding more and more," Fiona said before letting Zara go and kindly smiling at her that she wasn't used to seeing. Fiona always had an aura of superiority around her that it was almost unnerving to see her softer side coming through. Zara looked at her with a slight frown before going back to her desk, but Fiona's words were ringing in her ears. Zara thought back to the conversations she and Gill had, the way Gill had gotten Zara to write down the things she was happy to let her take over. It didn't feel like a power strip. It felt nice not to have to think about all the bills as they had a joint bank account in which both their pays went into. They both kept $800 a month for themselves, which they could spend any way they wanted. Zara had told Gill that she could be in charge of the food they ate, and she had never eaten better in her life. Gill had even helped her to buy a new car, letting Zara put her name on the insurance and ownership so that the premiums would be lower. Sure, Zara could see how, in a toxic relationship that there could be an abuse of power, but that wasn't Gill. She was a good person. She wasn't like that.

Zara brushed off the thoughts Fiona had put in her head, deciding that Fiona was probably just jealous as she got back on with her job.

Zara arrived home before Gill and collected the mail from the mailbox. It wasn't much, but it was something Zara loved doing because it made her feel grounded, that this was her home, and she belonged here. Gill had bought the house when they wanted to move in together. Zara had felt bad that she wasn't able to contribute much to the deposit, feeling spoilt and slightly embarrassed when Gill still put her name on the ownership paperwork. They had planted a strip of lavender up the garden path to the front door, and as Zara walked toward the door, she put out her hand and let it sweep past the lavender. They had planted it because of the bees it attracted, and on more than one occasion, Zara had been stung. For her, it was worth the risk. The warm afternoon sun shone down, warming Zara's hair by the time she arrived at the door, taking out her key but noticing the door was already unlocked. She frowned, everything in her body telling her not to go inside, she took out her phone and called Gill, happy when she heard her phone ringing inside. Still hesitant, she waited for Gill to pick up the phone.

"Hey baby," Gill happily said, making Zara walk into the house.

"Hey," Zara replied, seeing Gill in the living room, a cardboard box on the couch.

"The door was unlocked, I didn't think you would be home this early," Zara replied, putting her bag down and walking over to Gill, collapsing on the couch and kicking her heels off.

"I know that you have been struggling to maintain your fitness routine, so I thought this might help," Gill said, tilting her head toward the box. Zara looked at her suspiciously, peeping into the box, and squealing with excitement.

"A puppy!" Zara exclaimed, taking the German Shepherd puppy out of the box.

"A guy at work had a litter and asked if I wanted one. She's been vet check, and she's in great condition. You can call her anything you want," Gill said, watching as the puppy excitedly licked Zara all over.

"Mommy, I love her!" Zara said, disregarding the last trace of fear from her mind that Gill was an overbearing partner.

"Anything I want?" Zara asked, causing Gill to smirk.

"As long as it's not a silly name," Gill replied, stroking the dog's soft coat. Zara thought for a moment, snuggling into Gill and letting the puppy climb over the top of them. "Okay,   what about Freya?" Zara asked, playing with the puppy's paws. She felt Gill kiss the top of her head.

"Freya it is," Gill said, surprised at how much the name suited the dog.

"So, I bought a few things that she'll need. You can take her for a walk now if you want, or a run?" Gill said, making Zara frown. Sure, she hadn't exercised in a while, but it seemed that Gill was trying to say something.

"And if I don't?" Zara said, as Gill got up and took the dog leash out of the bag.

"Well, we agreed that you would work out every day. So if you don't, you'll get this on your ass," Gill said, putting up her hands.

"Your choice," she said, as Zara reached out and took the leash, clipping it onto Freya's collar and putting her on the ground.

"Fine," Zara said, Gill just raising an eyebrow and heading into the bathroom to have a shower.

After that day, Zara couldn't shake the feeling that

Gill was trying to take too much of her autonomy. She tried to ignore it, being annoyed when Gill controlled her little outfits at night even though she had been the one to suggest it in the first place.

Maybe I'm just moody tonight or something? Zara thought to herself, fussing and testing Gill's patience.

"I don't wanna!" Zara yelled as Gill pulled her arm through the onesie.

"You're on your way to getting your ass spanked, little one," Gill sternly said as she rolled Zara onto her tummy and gave her a taste of what she could expect.

"But Mommy," Zara whined, trying to shield her ass from Gill's firm hand, with no avail.

"No. You've been a brat for days, and I am not putting up with it anymore," Gill replied, grabbing Zara by the upper arm and dragging her into the living room.

"Stand there," Gill said, turning Zara around and making her face the wall. Taking her wrists and putting them behind her back, Gill began to walk away.

"Don't you fucking dare of think of moving. You can stay there until you decide to be a good girl for Mommy," Gill said, turning the light off and going back into the bedroom.

Well, at least I'm not getting spanked, Zara thought as she sighed deeply.
Gill sat at the edge of their bed and put her head in her hands.

What the fuck is going on? She thought to herself, disappointed at how the last few days had been. She thought back to all the times Zara had complained about following the tasks and boundaries that they had both agreed to and sighed.

Maybe work is really hard for her right now or something? Gill continued to guess, trying to figure out how their perfect world had turned so sour almost overnight. She was worried that her relationship with Zara was fast becoming like the relationship she had experienced time after time where everything was fine until it wasn't. As she lay on top of the bed, she knew that she needed to talk to Zara, but she wasn't sure how. When she had spoken to her about her concerns on other topics, Gill felt as though Zara would hide her true feelings and just agree to whatever Gill said. Gill rolled over and checked her phone. Zara had been out there for ten minutes, so Gill got up and walked out into the living room.

"Baby girl?" Gill asked as she turned on the light and looked at Zara.

"I'm sorry, Mommy," Zara said, feeling Gill come and cuddle her from behind.

"I know you are, baby girl," Gill said, sitting down and pulling Zara into her lap. Gill wrapped her arms around Zara and rocked her gently, wondering how to bring the issue up.

"Are you happy with how things have been this last week?" Gill asked, Zara, turning around in her arms.

"Yes, why?" Zara said, making Gill hold her breath.

"Because I think you're lying," Gill said,

biting her bottom lip. Zara looked like she had just been busted sneaking a cookie she wasn't meant to be eating.

"Um, no. Why would I lie?" She replied. In her heart, she knew that she wanted to talk about her feelings. She just didn't know what words she should be saying. Gill sighed and pulled her knees up to her chest.

"It's just that. You can't tell me this week hasn't felt a bit. I don't know. A bit weird. Like you are pulling away from me. Am I doing something wrong?" Gill asked. Zara both loved and hated that Gill was so good at seeing her for all that she was, and she rolled her eyes and sighed.

"I just think that maybe I gave away too much power, and I want some of it back," Zara said, feeling the knot in her stomach tighten. She had always hated confrontation and had actively tried to avoid it. But she had slowly realized that there was a difference between avoiding confrontation and denying her own reality.

"Oh, really. Okay, then let's talk about what

things you want control over then," Gill said, making Zara burst into tears. She hadn't thought that Gill would be so supportive, and she crawled into Gill's lap and cried into her chest.

"It's alright, sweetheart. Did you think I was going to get mad at you?" Gill lovingly asked as she rocked Zara. Zara just nodded her head as Gill soothed her.

Chapter 10

Zara wished that she didn't feel this way. It had been two weeks since she and Gill had decided on what Zara was going to reclaim control over, but she still felt as though something was not right. She looked over at Gill, who was sleeping next to her, wondering how much longer they would be together.

It's not even that she's bad or anything. I'm so lucky to have a Mommy, and I still feel this way, Zara thought to herself. She knew that she should be happy with Gill, but something just didn't feel right. It wasn't that she was doing something wrong, but something was missing. Gill stirred, causing Zara to beg that she wouldn't wake up.

I think I need to break up with her, she thought to herself before closing her eyes and squeezing them tight, trying not to burst out crying.

"Baby girl, Mommy's home," Gill called as she walked into the house. She dropped her bag by the door and smiled as she heard music coming from their bedroom. Walking down the hall, Gill slowly took her scarf and coat off as she walked, stopping when she saw Zara in the middle of a huge pile of clothes.

"Mommy," Zara said, looking up at Gill, surprised to see her home so early. Zara commanded the music to stop and scrunched up her face.

"I didn't think you'd be home so early," Zara apologetically said as she turned and looked at the huge mess on the floor.

"I can see that. What have you been up?" Gill said, putting her things away before sitting on the bed. Zara got up to join her, placing her hand on Gill's thigh as she snuggled into her.

"I wanted to find some new outfits, but I can't seem to make anything look good," Zara said with annoyance in her voice. Gill tried to suppress a smirk as she saw Zara's pouty face.

"Well. What sort of look were you going for?" Gill gently asked, sensing that this was a delicate topic.

"I don't know!" Zara dramatically exclaimed before she threw herself down onto the bed. Gill rubbed her back as she listened to Zara yell into the pillow.

"Okay, come on, show Mommy what sort of outfits you like," Gill said, deciding that Zara had been given enough time to feel sorry for herself. Zara let out a loud sigh and sat up, passing Gill her phone. Gill looked at the outfit styles as she flicked through the screenshots and nodded her head as she became more and more aware of the look Zara was trying to achieve.

"Okay. So, let's get all these clothes off the floor and see what we have to work with," Gill said, putting the phone down.

"But I've already tried that," Zara whined, getting a look from Gill.

"Move it," Gill said, pointing to the clothes.

Zara got off the bed reluctantly and began to put the clothes on the bed. When she was finished, Gill helped her sort the clothes into the different looks, making a list of the things that Zara needed to complete the look.

"Thanks, Mommy," Zara quietly said as she snuggled into Gill, looking at the bed with all of the outfit choices.

"It's okay," Gill said, kissing the top of Zara's head and passing her a handful of coat hangers.

"Now put everything back on these and come out to the living room. I'm going to make a start with dinner," Gill said, patting Zara on the ass.

"Little one," Gill said, coming into the kitchen an hour later. Zara sat at the bench, her stomach in knots.

"I think we need to break up," Zara blurted out, taking Gill by surprise. Gill stopped walking and froze. This was not what she was expecting.

"Um, why?" Gill asked, coming to sit by

Zara. Gill's hair falling to one side.

"Because I don't think this is working for me anymore, it just feels flat," Zara said, bursting into tears. Gill sighed and looked around the room, trying to process what Zara was telling her.

"It can get like this sometimes," Gill said, standing up and making herself a coffee. She looked out the window and rubbed her breasts as she waited for the water to boil in the kettle.

"I don't want to lose you," Gill said once the light went off, signaling that the water was ready for the coffee sachet.

"I know, I don't want to lose you either, but I also don't want to keep feeling this way. I don't know what I'm looking for, but I just feel like I can't get into little space with you at the level I want and need," Zara said, wishing that she didn't have to have this conversation.

"So, do you want to try and work through this, or do you want to go our separate ways?" Gill said, coming to sit down next to Zara.

"I kinda want to go our separate ways, but I

really don't want it to be like a mean break up. I don't want to get into a fight with you," Zara fearfully said, making Gill tilt her head to the side.

"Zara. I am not going to get mean with you, sweetie! Of course, I am sad that we are ending this, but I'm not going to make it any harder than it is already going to be," Gill said, feeling her heartbreak.

"I can move out if you need me too. I can pay my half of the rent for the rest of the contract if you want," Zara said, feeling somewhat relieved that Gill was so civil.

"You can stay as long as you want Zara, I'm not about to kick you out onto the street," Gill laughed buttoning up her pajama skirt. Zara noticed the subtle way she was pulling away emotionally.

What were you expecting? She needs to protect herself as well, Zara thought to herself.

"I might move into the spare room tonight if that's cool?" Zara said, Gill just nodding her head and quickly standing up, going over to the sink and putting her coffee cup down.

"Do you want help? If not, I might go out tonight," Gill said, sadly looking at Zara.

"No, it's cool. I can do it myself," Zara said, Gill, forcing a smile and walking into their bedroom.

Fuck. I hope this was the right decision, Zara said to herself as she sat in the kitchen by herself.

Chapter 11

"Thanks for coming," Zara said as she opened the door to Fiona. Fiona stood in the doorway with her usual flamboyant outfit and resting bitch face.

"Anytime, I told you that," Fiona replied, suddenly changing into the sweet and kind person Zara had learned that she could be when the situation arose. Zara smiled, moved out of the way, and waited for Fiona to come inside, closing the door behind her.

"So, what's going on?" Fiona said, sitting in the living room and seeing the afternoon tea that Zara had set on the coffee table. Gill hadn't come home last night. She had text Zara saying that she would be staying with a friend for a few days. So Zara had invited Fiona over. Zara wasn't really sure what she expected from the afternoon, but she just knew that she needed a friend who understood what she was going through. Zara sat down on the couch, offering Fiona tea and cake and serving her before she got into the details as to why Fiona had been invited over.

"So. Things haven't been the best between Gill and I lately," Zara said, running her hand through her hair. Fiona raised an eyebrow.

"But you always seem so happy at work?" She questioned, enjoying the red velvet cake Zara had made. Zara sighed, nodding her head and wondering how she was going to explain the situation.

"I know. And for the most part, it is great. But, and I'm not blaming you, but ever since you asked if I was giving too much of myself up, I have felt all, I don't know, weird," Zara said, shaking her head and being disappointed that she wasn't able to articulate her feelings any better. Fiona looked shocked and disappointed.

"I'm so sorry. I didn't mean for you to take it like there was something wrong with how you guys were doing stuff," Fiona said, putting her plate down and looking concerned.

"You know I say stuff off the cuff," Fiona added, taking a sip of her tea.

"Yeah, I know. But I think you were right. And now, I just don't want the dynamic to continue to go the way it was going. I, I kinda don't want to be her baby anymore, and so I broke up with her, but I don't even know if that was right decision either," Zara said, putting her hand over her mouth after she heard herself. Fiona just shrugged her shoulders. Clearly, she didn't find this to be as shocking as Zara had.

"Then tell her that. Who cares if you don't want to be her baby anymore? That's ok, just break up with her. It's better to make a clean cut than to drag it out and cause both of you unnecessary heartbreak. But if you want to be with her, you better find a good apology gift," Fiona said, looking at Zara expectantly. Zara crossed her legs on the couch and thought for a moment.

"And that's the thing, I still like a lot of what

we do, I just, I don't know, I want more control," Zara half yelled, getting frustrated, which made Fiona smirk.

"Have you thought about how much of a moody teen you sound like?" Fiona asked, the look on her face making Zara annoyed.

"Why do you find this so funny?!" Zara yelled, storming off into the kitchen to get a glass of water before coming back and sitting back down.

"Look. Has it occurred to you that maybe, just maybe, you are more of a middle than a little? And that maybe you felt more little when you had to care of yourself, but now that you have a Mommy and don't need to do everything yourself, you feel a little bit bigger?" Fiona asked, coming over to sit next to Zara, wrapping her arm around her.

"No," Zara said, the pout on her face making Fiona laugh.

"Maybe try it out, see if you like it. You can still wear diapers. You can still snuggle with a paci and a bottle, you can still have your train set, for example. But you can also do other things like deciding what you want to wear, what you want to eat, how much you work out, maybe have some different hobbies. I don't know, all I'm saying is that maybe you shouldn't limit yourself and therefore your relationship to just one thing. I like to think of it all as more of a spectrum and depending on the day, depends on how far along the spectrum you want to swing. If that makes sense?" Fiona said, smiling as she felt Zara reach out and hug her tightly.

"Thank you," Zara said, wishing she knew how she was going to word this so that Gill understood what she wanted.

After Fiona left, Zara finished moving her belongings into the spare bedroom.

I didn't realize how much stuff I had, Zara, though, as she collected the last of her things from their old bedroom just as she heard Gill coming home. Quickly running into her new room, Zara dumped the armful of little things on the bed before walking out to the living room.

"Hey," she said, seeing Gill coming through the door with two big shopping bags.

"Hi," Gill replied, putting the bags down on the kitchen bench, without looking at Zara.

"I moved my stuff out," Zara said as they looked at each other awkwardly.

"Okay, great," Gill said, feeling her stomach knot as she began to put the groceries away.

"Can I help?" Zara said, Gill, sighing and putting a bag of pasta down on the bench before turning to look at Zara.

"Yeah, sure," Gill sighed, before turning back toward the pantry.

"Look. This is going to get really hard before it gets better," Gill suddenly said. She had spent the day at a café, thinking about Zara, where their relationship had gone wrong and generally licking her wounds. It had been what she needed to spend the time to try and process the feelings she was feeling, but nothing had prepared her to feel the disappointment she now felt.

"I think maybe it would be good if you moved out. As I said, I'm not going to kick you out. I'll help you find a place if you like. I'm not just going to dump you on your ass, but I think it would be better for me if you were happy to move out," Gill said, wishing that she didn't feel the emotional pull toward Zara. Zara just nodded her head. She understood where Gill was coming from and didn't want to make it any harder for her than it would be already.

"That makes sense. I can look for a place tomorrow," Zara said, fake smiling. Gill returned the gesture, and they both stood in the kitchen in silence, looking at each other.

"This sucks," Gill laughed, shaking her head, enjoying a moment of relief from her broken heart.

"Yeah, I know. I'm sorry I was the one to do it," Zara said, feeling guilty. Gill just shrugged her shoulders.

"It happens. Maybe if I had given you more attention or done something differently, it wouldn't be the case, but it is so," Gill said, Zara, tearing up and shaking her head.

"I don't think so. I don't think it had anything to do with you or me doing or not doing something. I just think we want different things," Zara said, causing Gill to tilt her head in curiosity.

"What do you mean?" Gill said, feeling herself have a faint glimmer of hope in her heart that she could get Zara back.

"Like. I like diapers and baby stuff, but I kinda don't at the same time," Zara said, causing Gill to roll her eyes.

"Oh my fucking god, are you kidding me?" Gill said, raising her voice and somewhat starling Zara.

"What?" Zara defensively replied, feeling attacked.

"Maybe, you are more of a middle than a little? That could explain why you don't want super baby things anymore. Maybe I did such a great fucking job of looking after you that you moved up in your little age. It happens sometimes.

I read about it," Gill said, rolling her eyes. Zara smirked for a moment, enjoying that the Mommies in her life understood things that had clearly escaped her.

"Would you be interested in trying it out with me?" Zara asked, making Gill laugh.

"Fuck me, darling. You sure know how to turn my life absolutely inside fucking out," Gill said, making Zara laugh.

"Sure, why the hell not. Let's try it for a while and see if it's something we both like," Gill said, feeling her heart pounding in her chest as the emotional turmoil that she had experienced all day caught up with her.

"Can you stay in the spare room tonight, though? I need a minute to process everything," Gill said, taking out a bottle of wine and pouring two glasses.

"Here," Gill said, shaking her head as Zara laughed.

"Sorry," Zara genuinely said, feeling embarrassed, apologetic, and relieved at Gill's response. Gill laughed and shook her head.

"I feel so sick," Gill said, going to the couch and laying down. She put her arm over her eyes and sighed, letting the feeling wash over her.

"Can I be honest?" Zara asked, making Gill laugh.

"I think I can only take so much of your honesty for one day," Gill replied, feeling Zara sit down on the floor and put her face close to Gill's thigh.

"I didn't think you liked me that much," Zara whispered, causing Gill to sit up and look at her with a shocked expression on her face.

"What do you mean?" Gill questioned, surprised that Zara would feel that way.

"Well, like I just didn't feel like you did. I thought you weren't like super into me or whatever," Zara said, Gill, feeling like she was losing her mind.

"Mommy needs another drink," Gill said, getting up, Zara watching her from the floor.

"Zara. I fucking adore you," Gill said, taking

a sip and coming back to the couch with her glass in one hand and the bottle in the other.

"Damn, we really have a few things we need to work on," Gill said as she drank. Zara just laughed.

"Have you heard of love languages?" Zara asked, watching as Gill placed her glass down.

"Not really," Gill replied. Zara stood up and moved to the couch, sitting down next to Gill and taking out her phone.

"Okay, so it's like everyone has their own love language. You can do a test to figure out which one is yours. Mine is gifts. So I feel most loved when I get gifts," Zara explained. Gill wrapped her arm around Zara, smiling when Zara snuggled into her.

"I think yours will be affection but do you want to do the test and find out? That way, we can start to do stuff that speaks the other person's love language?" Zara suggested, smiling as Gill nodded her head and took the phone in her hands.

Chapter 12

"How are you going?" Gill's friend Mike asked her a week later. Gill learned that her love language was primarily quality time, so she and Zara had tried to incorporate both of their love languages into their dynamic. Their dynamic had also taken on a different tone, with Zara doing a lot of different things such as listening to music more frequently, learning dances, and watching shows that were more stimulating than her previous cartoons.

"It's been good. I must say, it took a minute to feel better after she 'broke up' with me. I kind of felt like I didn't want to give her another chance because I was hurting, but when I realized that it was just her cute, dumb ass freaking out about not knowing how to communicate, I got over it," Gill explained making Mike laugh.

"I really don't know how you do it. I mean, I

would lose my mind if somebody like Zara had me on an emotional roller coast like that," Mike said, taking a sip of his coffee. Gill just laughed.

"Yeah, but it's not like she does it on purpose. I really don't think she can help being a little bit, I don't want to use the word unstable, but I mean, she's learning how to control her emotions and learning about herself, and that sort of thing takes a while to figure out," Gill replied shrugging her shoulders. She smiled to herself, understanding that it was okay that Mike had no idea how she could manage it. The thing was, Gill didn't feel like she was simply managing. She felt as though as she was helping build and maintain her relationship with Zara.

"I mean, relationships take time to build, they change, and they develop. How boring if everyone just stayed the same. I'm happy that we are in a situation where we can build on our foundation. I'm in this for the long haul with her," Gill said, making Mike wonder if it was herself that she was telling this too and not him.

"I get that. But is that how Zara feels? If she was so quick to break up with you, maybe she isn't in it for the long haul like you are?" Mike asked. Gill thought about the comment for a moment before shaking her head.

"No, she is, she just never had somebody who was prepared to stay with her as she went through growth periods. She thought that the best way to evolve was to leave," Gill explained. Mike just shrugged his shoulder and made a face that told Gill that he accepted her answer, even if he didn't really understand it. Gill smiled as well and looked out the window, excited to get home to Zara. They had decided to spend the weekend in Gill's cabin in the woods and Gill knew that she wanted to get home before sundown.

The wind was blowing stronger than Gill had thought it would as she looked out over the rolling hills. As the sun came down and the sky shone in muted hues of pinks and purples, she knew that she needed to get inside and start the fire.

"Zara?" Gill called as she passed the horses of her neighbour and walked inside. She had stayed with Mike longer than she had thought she would, and was worried that Zara would be a hangry little mess by the time she saw her. Shutting the wooden door to the cabin, Gill shivered as she looked around.

"Baby?" Gill called again, as she saw Zara walking out of their bedroom with her earphones in, startling when she saw Gill.

"Mommy!" Zara exclaimed, holding onto her chest.

"Oh my gosh, feel my heartbeat," Zara said as she ran over to the older woman. Gill smirked as Zara pulled up her t-shirt and placed Gill's hand on her chest.

"I have a sneaky feeling you want me to feel more than just your heartbeat," Gill said as she groped Zara's breasts, making her giggle.

"Maybe," Zara said, pulling back slightly when she saw the look in Gill's eye.

"So, have you done your chores?" Gill asked,

looking around the living space. Zara beamed up at her, before running over to the fridge and taking her sticker chart in her hands and coming back over to Gill who was busy lighting the fire.

"Yep. See," Zara said, holding it up proudly. Gill looked over the sheet and smiled, patting Zara on the ass lovingly.

"I think that you need some new stickers," Gill said, taking it from Zara's hands and putting it back on the fridge. Zara was standing next to the fire, Freya coming to lay on the rug in front of it and warmed herself as Zara listened to Gill.

"Can we go into town to get them tomorrow, please, Mommy?" Zara said, turning her hands over as Gill came to stand behind her. Wrapping her arms around Zara's body, Gill rested her head on Zara's shoulder and kissed her cheek affectionately.

"We have to see. Mommy has a few things to do tomorrow," Gill replied, Zara, trying not to feel disappointed that it wasn't a straight yes. Nodding her head, Zara turned around in Gill's arms and snuggled into her breasts.

"What is it, baby girl? You've been a bit off all day, haven't you?" Gill questioned. Zara had spent the day trying to fight herself to remain happy and feeling balanced, but the day hadn't gone to plan at all, which meant her routine had been thrown into disarray. Usually, when this happened, she could just go for a run and almost reset herself, but as the winter winds had picked up early this year, the bite of the cold was too much to bear.

"I don't know. I just feel so, yuck," Zara said, sighing deeply.

"I don't want to feel like this, but I just don't feel right," she added, sitting down on the couch.

"Well. How about Mommy takes you out for takeout, and then we can come back and watch a movie?" Gill asked, hoping that would be enough to make her little one smile again.

"I'd like that. I just hate feeling this way," Zara said. Getting up, Zara walked into the mudroom and put her boots on. Gill had decided to keep the fire burning, and while they were out, Freya laying comfortably on her rug as the house warmed.

"My little snow bunny," Gill said, seeing the pink bandana Zara was putting on over her ears, it matched her blonde her perfectly.

"Burgers and shakes?" Gill asked, knowing that she would need to go for an extra-long hike the next morning to work it off.

"Perfect," Zara said, standing by the door. Although she was only eight years younger than Gill, Zara's youthful appearance kept Gill in Mommy space almost permanently. Looking at her beautiful girl waiting by the door, Gill knew why. Zara's long, wavy blonde hair, her tight figure, and firm but generous curves looked divine in her adult clothes and her little clothes. Gill smirked, wondering if Zara was in the mood for some playtime and grabbed the back of her jeans, pulling her back into her.

"Why have you got big girl panties on, baby girl?" Gill whispered in Zara's ear, roughly rubbing her through the front of her jeans. Gill loved how Zara instinctively began to bite her bottom lip and accept Gill's touch.

"Because I had to go into town today, Mommy," Zara replied, bending over and placing her hands on the wall as Gill unbuttoned the front of her jeans and cupped her pussy. Gill's hands were cold, and she smiled as she heard Zara gasp and try to get away from her touch.

"Where do you think you're going?" Gill said, pushing Zara's panties into her pussy and rubbing her gently. Zara just moaned as she was toyed with, feeling Gill's hand on the back of her head, keeping her face against the wall.

"Take these off, Mommy is going to put you in something more appropriate," Gill ordered, standing back and folding her arms across her chest. Zara turned around slowly, looking up at Gill with her innocent eyes as she obeyed her commands. Her jeans fell to the floor, Zara bending down to pick them up and hand them to Gill, who had her hand out waiting. Next, Zara slowly slid her panties off, her legs getting goose bumps as they were exposed.

"Go lay on Mommy's bed," Gill said, as Zara handed her her panties, before following the instruction. Zara walked into their room, crawled up onto the high bed, and waited for Gill. She knew what was coming, and she felt butterflies of anticipation in her stomach as she waited. Gill loved diapering her when they were going out for small trips, enjoying how it made Zara feel small and cling to her. Usually, Gill would put her in a pull-up, so that Zara could still wear her skinny jeans over the top, but tonight Gill had something else planned.

"We aren't getting out of the car tonight. So," Gill said, taking out a thick diaper and almost giving Zara a heart attack.

"Mommy, I can't wear that! What if someone sees me?" Zara questioned, her eyes going wide as she tried to protest.

"Now, listen to me. If someone sees you, they are just going to think what a sweet little girl you are," Gill replied, enjoying the resistance in Zara's squirming body.

"Stay still for Mommy, or you'll get a spanking, and it'll still go on, is that what you want?" Gill said, placing the thick, crinkly diaper under Zara who just pouted.

"It's not fair," Zara whined, making Gill smirk. Zara crossed her arms over her chest and pouted as Gill sprinkled fresh baby powder over her and stuck the tabs of the diaper down.

"There, doesn't that feel nice, baby girl?" Gill questioned, going into the cupboard and taking out Zara's pink sweatpants and pulling them up and over her diaper. Rubbing her hands over the pants, Gill enjoyed watching as Zara resisted the pull into little space, deciding that she was going to be a brat instead.

"You know, I'm not happy with how snarky you've been tonight," Gill whispered in Zara's ear as she took her wrist and pulled her into the corner.

"So you can stand here until you fix that

attitude, young lady," Gill said, putting socks onto Zara's feet before turning her body to face the wall. Zara just sighed dramatically before crossing her arms over her chest and resting her weight on one foot.

"Oh, is that what you thought you'd be doing with your hands?" Gill said, taking Zara's wrists and tying them behind her back, pulling them tightly.

"Mommy!" Zara whined, her little voice escaping and making her pout in defeat.

"That's better," Gill said, patting Zara on the top of her head before walking out of the room and leaving Zara to stand in the corner. Gill walked out to the living room and sat down, enjoying how warm the space was, and she lay down on the couch and took out her phone. Flicking through social media, she came across an account that had some half-decent content. Gill smiled as she scrolled through the photos and stopped when she saw a few scenes that she knew she wanted to explore with Zara. Putting her phone down, Gill got off the couch and walked back to the bedroom and looked Zara in the eye.

"Still feeling like you want to be bratty for Mommy?" Gill asked, already knowing the answer.

"No, Mommy," Zara said, shaking her head and looking up at Gill and trying to grab at her wanting to be held.

"Good girl," Gill said as she opened her arms and held onto Zara, who snuggled into her like her life depended on it.

"You know, Mommy had a few ideas while you were fixing your attitude," Gill said with a wicked grin that told Zara everything she needed to know.

"Mommy," Zara whined as she watched as Gill took off her shirt, knowing that she was in for a wild ride.

"Oh yes, that's exactly what I want to hear, little girl," Gill replied, cupping Zara's chin in her hand and forcing her eyes to look up at her. Zara felt Gill begin to grab at her sweat pants, pulling them down roughly, Zara kicking them off.

"I don't know why I didn't just do this in the first place," Gill said, sitting down and bending Zara over her knee.

"Girls who are rude need to be taught a lesson," Gill said as she spanked Zara firmly, leaving red handprints all over her thighs and making her ass sting, even though the diaper. Zara knew that she needed to stay quiet, or she'd get extra spanks, but as Gill landed the final blow, she yelped.

"Oh, you know what that means," Gill said, taking a gag from the bookshelf and pushing it into Zara's mouth, securing it around her neck and continuing to spank her. Zara wriggled on Gill's lap, causing Gill to hold her down with her forearm as she spanked Zara's thighs.

"If you had been a good girl, instead of a bratty little slut, I wouldn't have to do this," Gill said, enjoying being able to be more firm and aggressive with Zara's punishments. Zara stopped thrashing around on Gill's lap, making Gill begin to rub Zara's diapered ass and thighs between spanks, eventually slowing them down until she was only stroking Zara. Taking the gag from her mouth, Gill pushed Zara to the ground and pulled her panties off before bringing Zara's mouth to her pussy.

"Don't make me wait," Gill said, holding Zara firmly in place as she began to lap at Gill's cunt with enthusiasm.

"There's my good girl. Did your moody little ass need to be reminded who was in charge?" Gill moaned as Zara expertly fucked her.

"Put your hands behind your back," Gill instructed, pulling Zara's head back to slap her cheek.

"And look up at me," Gill commanded, looking down into Zara's eyes and was edged closer and closer. Zara could feel herself slowly coming out of this space and wanting this to stop, grateful when Gill came quickly, pulling her head backward.

"Mommy," Zara softly said, Gill, looking down to see Zara needed to stop.

"It's ok, sweetie. Mommy is here," Gill said, picking Zara up from the floor and bringing her into her arms. Gill hadn't been so rough with Zara before and knew that their dinner plans would need to wait.

"Shh, Mommy's here," Gill cooed, feeling Zara snuggle into her.

"Bath and quiet time?" Gill said Zara nodding.

"Maybe a shower, though," Zara replied, Gill, smiling to herself. She was still adjusting to Zara feeling more grown-up than the little she had first been when they started their relationship.

"Okay. Do you want me stay or go?" Gill asked as they walked to the shower.

"You can stay," Zara said, turning on the water before undressing herself. Gill sat on the wooden stool in the bathroom and watched as Zara put her clothes in the wash basket, set her diaper aside and stepped into the shower. The water ran down her body, and Gill smiled to herself as she looked at her beautiful girlfriend.

"I think I want my new pajamas. Tonight, Mommy, but like, a diaper still, for when we go out," Zara said from the shower.

"Could you get them for me, please?" She added, smiling at she saw Gill stand up.

"Sure, sweetie," Gill said before walking into the bedroom. She took down a diaper and rummaged through Zara's section of the cupboard before finding the pajamas she wanted just as Zara walked into the room.

"Can Mommy do it for you?" Gill asked, holding up the diaper, happy when Zara nodded.

"Okay, lay up here for me then, princess," Gill said, patting the stop on the bed that she wanted Zara to lay down. Obediently, Zara moved to where Gill wanted her and moved her body at Gill's command while she was diapered.

"I can do this myself, though," Zara said, putting her pajamas on and putting her hair in a messy ponytail.

"You're a cutie, baby girl," Gill said, as Zara snuggled into her, coming to sit in her lap. Zara took out her phone and gave Gill an AirPod before turning on a movie.

"Yeah, I might be a big girl, but I will always need Mommy's cuddles," Zara said, as Gill ordered their dinner online and turned off the light as the movie began.

The end... not quite!

To receive your free Baby Fox Coloring In, visit the link:

www.tinamooreauthor.com

Who is Tina Moore?

Tina Moore has enjoyed the lifestyle of a Mommy Domme for several years. She began secretly exploring kink and BDSM in her youth and found her love of being a strict Mommy Domme in early 2000. Tina Moore slowly became more comfortable and confident through making friends in the community and exploring the lifestyle and now openly celebrates being a Mommy Domme to her little.

Before becoming an author, Tina Moore worked in the finance sector, but it was through the encouragement of her current little that she took the leap and wrote her first MDLG book, Nancy's Little One.

From then on, Tina Moore continued to combine her experiences and desires, as well as the sweet and naughty things her baby girl does, to bring you tantalizing and salacious stories about both MDLG and DDLG relationships and the ABDL littles and middles who enjoy them.

Follow her on:

Author Page on Amazon

Instagram @tinamoore.kdp